The Happy Hunter

A Comedy in Three Acts

by Georges Feydeau

English Adaptation by Barnett Shaw

THE HAPPY HUNTER, by Georges Feydeau, English adaptation by Barnett Shaw, 7 M., 3 W., 2 Int., 1900 period France. Chandel tells Yvonne he is going hunting with Castillo, but when Castillo turns up unexpectedly, she sees the hoax, and therefore decides to yield to Roussel's amorous advances, going to his bachelor den with him. But, across the hall, Chandel is having a rendezvous with Madame Castillo. A hectic evening ensues, complicated by an eccentric landlady and by the appearance of Yvonne's nephew, whose girl friend used to live there. The police, seeking Madame Castillo's lover, grab Roussel, while Chandel escapes through the window and runs off with Roussel's trousers. The mix-up unravels in act three, with one surprise after the other, Yvonne winning all tricks while her husband gets the punishment.

CHARACTERS
(*As They Appear*)

Roussel, *a doctor, who has amorous designs upon*

Yvonne Chandel, *who is the wife of his best friend,*

Chandel, *the happy hunter.*

Babette, *the maid in the Chandel home, and*

Pierre, *a student, and nephew to the Chandels.*

Castillo, *who comes from Guatemala.*

Madame de Latour, *an old aristocrat, now a concierge.*

Inspector Duval, *of the Paris police, and naturally,*

First Policeman, *who doesn't like to be called "un flic,"*

Second Policeman, *who doesn't like to be called "un cognard."*

Place: *Paris*

Time: *Circa 1900*

ACT ONE

The study of Monsieur Chandel.

ACT TWO

Apartment of Roussel, 35 Avenue Gambetta.

ACT THREE

Same as Act One.

CHARACTERS

YVONNE, *a rather naive and gullible wife, very sweet and sincere.*

ROUSSEL, *suave and sensuous, very agile and impetuous.*

CHANDEL, *a philanderer, quite a story-teller. Tries to be very casual.*

PIERRE, *18, a student, breezy and alert.*

CASTILLO, *an amiable Latin, speaks with accent, fidgety and insecure.*

MADAME DE LATOUR, *50, quasi-elegant, but rather coarse.*

DUVAL, *any age. Very officious and business-like.*

BABETTE, *pretty, pert, vivacious, 18 to 20.*

POLICEMEN, *may be any age.*

ROUSSEL, YVONNE, CHANDEL *and* CASTILLO *may be played in late twenties, thirties, or forties, as long as their ages are consistent with each other.*

COSTUMES

1900–1910 period, France.

YVONNE: A stylish, attractive dress in each act. In Act Two she enters with a broad-brim velvet hat, veil, and full-length cloth coat.

ROUSSEL: Dark, pin-stripe suit with vest in Act One and Two. Must be wearing black gloves in Act Two entrance. Gray suit with vest in Act Three. Black hat in all three acts.

Chandel: Beginning of Act One he wears a belted sports jacket with plain contrasting trousers. During act he puts on a pair of brightly-colored plaid trousers. Puts on red hunting cap during act. He wears this costume throughout Act Two until he puts on Roussel's pin-stripe trousers. Act Two entrance he carries a gun case and has a cartridge belt slung over his shoulder. He wears same costume in Act Three until he changes to trousers which Babette brings in.

Castillo: Double-breasted gray suit in Act One and Act Three. Black hat, break-away cane.

Pierre: In Act One he wears plaid trousers exactly like those which Chandel puts on during the act. He has a contrasting sport coat and vest. Broad-brim hat. Same costume in Act Two, but he enters without his hat. In Act Three he wears a blue blazer with white trim, white vest, and gray, striped trousers. No hat.

Babette: Traditional maid's uniform of black with white apron and cap.

Latour: Gaudy, elaborate dress, of questionable taste. A great deal of cheap jewelry. Eccentric coiffure.

Duval: Plain black suit and vest, black hat, in both Act Two and Act Three. He may wear a trench-coat.

Policemen: Plain dark suits, no hats.

PRONUNCIATION

For consistency, and for French flavor, all characters should approximate correct French pronunciation in French words and proper names.

Most French words have the intermediate "a" sound (a) rather than the broad "a" in "father." Lips should be stretched, as in the sound "ee," and the jaw should not drop as in the broad "a."

Madame—(madam) Both syllables have intermediate "a." The accent is never on the first syllable as in the English word "madam."

Mademoiselle—(madmwazel) Only three syllables, not "ma-dem-wa-zel."

Monsieur—First syllable has sound of "a" in "sofa." Last syllable is almost like "ur" with lips rounded and no "r" being sounded.

Messieurs—Same, except that first syllable has sound of "e" in "get."

Avenue Gambetta—(avny), not "av-e-noo" as in English. The first syllable of "Gambetta" should be nasalized and not pronounced as in "ham."

Franc—This word should be slightly Americanized for proper understanding, pronouncing the final "c."

Duval—(Dyval) First syllable is like "ee" with lips rounded. Last syllable is intermediate "a" and not broad "a."

Roussel—(Rusel)

Chandel—The "ch" is like in "sugar." The "an" should be nasalized and not pronounced as in "hand."

Pâté—Here the "a" is broad as in "father." The final "ay" is not a diphthong.

Babette—First syllable is intermediate "a."

Concierge—First syllable is nasal. Ending is "air" with "s" as in "treasure."

Castillo—Kah-stee-yo, accent on next to last syllable.

Bon jour—First word is nasalized. The second word should not sound like "sure," but "oo" with an "r." "Bon jour" should be said with cheerful, upward inflection on the last word.

The Happy Hunter

ACT ONE

The study in the home of CHANDEL. *Double entry doors, rear, opening on hallway. Each side of door, a console or armchair. Down left, a desk with writing materials and small chair. To steady it, a thin book is under front leg nearest audience. Above desk, door leading to* CHANDEL'S *bedroom. Between desk and door, a hanging wicker birdcage which is empty. Down right, door leading to salon and* YVONNE'S *quarters. Above this door, a fireplace with pouf in front of it. Further upstage, a chair. In center of room, an oval table with chairs. Bell-cord by fireplace. As the play opens,* YVONNE *is seated right of table,* ROUSSEL, *left. They are stuffing cartridges. She adds the shot and wadding, he stuffs the material down and then crimps the cartridge. On the table is a cartridge stuffer, crimper, small hammer, cartridge pouch. Shot, powder, wadding are in small wooden bowls. There is a moment of silence.* ROUSSEL *looks at* YVONNE, *then back to cartridges, then speaks imploringly.*

ROUSSEL. Yvonne! Will you? (*Leans across the table, amorously.*) Oh, my dear Yvonne—tell me you will.

YVONNE. (*Shakes her head in negative while putting charge of shot in cartridge she holds.*) No! Let's get on with my husband's cartridges.

ROUSSEL. (*Rises, goes to* YVONNE, *holds his face close to hers.*) Yvonne, my love—say you will.

YVONNE. No! (*Hands him a cartridge.*) There! Stuff it, will you.

ROUSSEL. All right! I'll stuff it! (*Sits, furiously stuffing and crimping cartridge.*) After all, Yvonne—would it be so unpleasant for you?

YVONNE. (*Impatiently.*) Oh! (*Very categorically.*) No! No! No! There! Do you understand?

ROUSSEL. (*Annoyed, rises.*) Oh, that's fine—that's excellent! Do you realize I'm asking you for the first proof of our love?

YVONNE. The first? It seems to me you want to start with the final proof.

ROUSSEL. (*Disdainfully.*) Ah! You have everything in numerical order. (*Convinced of his right.*) What am I asking, after all? A very natural thing—between two people who are fond of each other. Your husband is going hunting. I'm his friend. It's quite normal to ask you to spend the evening with me.

YVONNE. (*Scoffing.*) Evening? And all night? And suddenly it's morning!

ROUSSEL. You'll be home early in the morning. Besides, I must be at my office at eight.

YVONNE. How you talk.

ROUSSEL. You have absolutely no confidence in me.

YVONNE. But, look here, foolish man, even if I wanted to—to do what you ask—think of my reputation. What would the servants say if I didn't come home all night? Oh, what babbling tongues.

ROUSSEL. (*With disdain.*) You look at things in a trivial way. (*He sits down again.*) As if a woman wouldn't know how to throw her servants off the track.

YVONNE. Oh, yes—you think it's easy. (*Passes a cartridge to* ROUSSEL.) Twenty-nine.

ROUSSEL. (*Taking cartridge and stuffing it.*) Twenty-nine. Don't you have a relative you could pretend to be visiting?

YVONNE. I have an aunt in the country.

ROUSSEL. Perfect! While your husband goes hunting, you are going to visit your aunt in the country. I'm sure the old dear will be very glad to see you.

YVONNE. No doubt! And while going to my aunt's, I make a detour to thirty-five Avenue Gambetta, where the bachelor retreat of Doctor Roussel happens to be.

ROUSSEL. (*Very sincere.*) That's exactly right!

YVONNE. (*Scoffing.*) Can you really imagine my going to your apartment?

ROUSSEL. (*With conviction.*) Of course! I see it very clearly.

YVONNE. You're joking.

ROUSSEL. I'm not joking. My apartment is very near here.

YVONNE. And that's a reason?

ROUSSEL. Yvonne, when I told you I was renting a little bachelor apartment today, you said: "Good—it's very near." Didn't you say that?

YVONNE. Perhaps.

ROUSSEL. You did—and my heart beat like a jungle drum. The apartment is being made ready for me this afternoon. There was a girl living there—her name was Fifi Limande—she couldn't pay her rent, so she was asked to leave.

YVONNE. I don't see the connection.

ROUSSEL. (*Bitterly.*) You see—we are two different natures. When you said: "Good—it's very near," I thought you meant— (*Very amorously.*) "Good—it's very near."

YVONNE. You must have a pretty opinion of me if you think I frequent bachelors' apartments.

ROUSSEL. (*Protesting.*) Me? Believe a thing like that? Of course not!

YVONNE. (*Passing a cartridge.*) Thirty.

ROUSSEL. (*Taking cartridge, stuffing it, and repeating mechanically.*) Thirty. (*Then with a new attack.*) Let's get back to my apartment.

YVONNE. We're not going back to your apartment.

ROUSSEL. (*Contritely.*) If I say "my apartment," it simply means "my home." Won't you step into my home?

YVONNE. You quibble on words. Let's not speak of it again.

ROUSSEL. (*Rises and paces the floor.*) I'm sorry I mentioned it in the first place.

YVONNE. Good! Smother your regrets and get your mind on the cartridges.

ROUSSEL. (*With mute anger.*) Oh, women! Women!

YVONNE. (*Indicating the cartridges.*) Are you finished?

ROUSSEL. Yes—I'm finished with the perverse creatures.

YVONNE. I was talking about the cartridges.

ROUSSEL. I'm finished with them, too. (*Holds up cartridge pouch.*) He has enough cartridges here. He's not going to kill every animal in the forest. Madame, I've had just about enough of stuffing cartridges for your husband. (*A change of tone.*) Oh, Yvonne, when I think how high I held you in my esteem—and you've let me fall—six floors at least. It hurts! But I can thank heaven that I saw you at last—standing naked before me.

YVONNE. What?

ROUSSEL. (*Sits again.*) A figure of speech.

YVONNE. I should hope so.

(CHANDEL *enters with shotgun, from* L., *coming between them, behind table. He is wiping gun with a cloth.*)

CHANDEL. Is everything going well?

ROUSSEL. Not at all.

CHANDEL. What's wrong?

ROUSSEL. Everything.

YVONNE. Nothing's wrong.

ROUSSEL. Speak for yourself—but for a person with my energetic nature, it's disheartening to see myself getting nowhere.

CHANDEL. Perhaps you're working too fast. Patience, my friend—you're not on a race-track.

ROUSSEL. Definitely not. I'm still in the stable.

CHANDEL. (*Good fellow.*) Could I be of help?

ROUSSEL. No—you would only be in the way.

CHANDEL. You're right. That's why I said to myself: "Roussel and my wife will do it quicker without my help."

ROUSSEL. Huh?

CHANDEL. It's really too small a matter to get upset about. You've done very well.

ROUSSEL. I have?

CHANDEL. Certainly. (*Looks in cartridge pouch.*) There are enough cartridges here for my hunt.

YVONNE. Thirty-one. (*She rises, takes pouch and places it on piece of furniture at* L.)

CHANDEL. You see, Roussel—you had nothing to worry about after all.

ROUSSEL. I'm glad you see it that way. (*Rises.*) But tell me, my friend, how can you enjoy hunting so much?

YVONNE. (*Promptly siding with* ROUSSEL.) Yes.

ROUSSEL. To see animals suffer! I can't—and I'm a man.

CHANDEL. Imagine a doctor talking like that.

ROUSSEL. I suppose you're going to the slaughter with your friend Castillo?

CHANDEL. Yes—as always.

ROUSSEL. We never see your friend Castillo.

YVONNE. No—we don't. (*She goes* L., *takes bag of sewing material and starts to work with yarn, seated at desk.*)

CHANDEL. Castillo has a lovely place in the country and he likes to stay there.

ROUSSEL. Where he can forget his matrimonial troubles, I suppose?

CHANDEL. He's separated from his wife, that's all. Their marriage difficulties started a few years after they moved here from Guatemala.

ROUSSEL. His wife has a lover.

CHANDEL. That hasn't been proved.

ROUSSEL. But everyone says so—that amounts to the same thing. Oh, I don't blame her. (*A pointed look at*

YVONNE.) The worthy woman has had one lover at least. (YVONNE *turns her head, pretending to pay no attention.*)

CHANDEL. (*Looking at* ROUSSEL, *not understanding.*) Why do you say "one lover at least"? You seem to infer that she has had several.

ROUSSEL. (*A little grumpy, as if it did not concern* CHANDEL.) I didn't mean it that way. I meant that she has at least had *a* lover.

CHANDEL. What do you really know about it? Is it because her husband says so? What does he know about it? Husbands are the last to know such things. He has ideas—yes—but no proof. And that's what enrages poor Castillo. If he had proof, he could get a divorce. But, excuse me, I must have this gun cleaned. (*He goes out, rear. There is a moment of silence.* ROUSSEL *paces,* YVONNE *works with her yarn.*)

ROUSSEL. (*Back to his fixed idea.*) Then, it's understood—for the third time—you won't come with me?

YVONNE. (*With a tiresome sigh.*) Again! No! That's final!

ROUSSEL. Are you sure?

YVONNE. Positive. (*She sits* L. *of table, with her needlework.*)

(*The following scene must be played by* ROUSSEL *with warmth and conviction, all the comedy being in his sincerity. . . . Feydeau's note.*)

ROUSSEL. (*Behind table.*) Good, good! But don't tell me again that you love me. (*Silence from* YVONNE, *he walks* L., *near the bird-cage.*) Because you did say it once! Remember your little parakeet that used to say so sweetly: (*Imitating a parakeet.*) "Yvonne, Yvonne, bitch, bitch." The dear little love-bird had just died, and the three of us were here—you and I and the dear departed. (*Profound sigh from* YVONNE.) Your husband had gone out. (*He crosses behind table, goes down* R. *of it. Speaks lyrically.*) You remember how you burst into tears? I consoled you—you cried on my shoulder. I held you in my arms, and my tears mingled with yours. (*Ordinary voice.*) I had put the parakeet on the pouf. (*Pantomimes the action then speaks lyrically again.*) At that very moment, you had one of those impulses of the heart that cannot lie. You looked into my eyes, and you said "I love you." I was mad with joy. Then—all of a sudden—your husband came in. I grabbed that damned parakeet just in time, and the three of us went on crying together.

YVONNE. I remember how I cried.

ROUSSEL. Then you can't deny that you said the "I love you" that started everything.

YVONNE. Who knows what one says in a moment of grief?

ROUSSEL. You were sincere at that moment—I swear to you. It's only during moments like that—when a woman isn't thinking of what she's saying—that a man can be sure she's saying what she's thinking.

YVONNE. But even if I did say "I love you," does that imply everything? Everything that is to follow? Really, I don't know what you see in it. (*She rises, goes* L.)

ROUSSEL. What do I see in it? Oh, la, la! (*Advances on her with a lascivious leer.*) What do I see in it!

YVONNE. (*Shocked.*) Oh!

ROUSSEL. (*Still moving toward her slowly.*) I mean to say, it's a pact—a bond—between two amorous people—a promissory note—with payment undetermined, but inevitable. Yes, Yvonne—as valuable as gold—with this one difference—it's not negotiable.

YVONNE. That's fortunate.

ROUSSEL. Oh, it's so easy to say "I love you." The difficult thing is to prove it. I'm ready to prove it. Are you?

YVONNE. (*Looks at him with a mocking air and then moves right.*) I protest the note!

ROUSSEL. You see! Breach of promise! How very unworthy of you.

YVONNE. (*Sitting at* R. *of table.*) What do you want of me, Roussel? There's a misunderstanding between us, that's all. You insist I said "I love you" while I was mourning for a loved one.

ROUSSEL. You said it. I couldn't mistake a thing like that.

YVONNE. I want very much to believe that I said it, and if I did, I promise you I won't go back on my word.

ROUSSEL. (*Triumphant.*) Do you mean that?

YVONNE. Of course. Why shouldn't my heart have the right to its preferences? After all, you don't displease me.

ROUSSEL. (*Vainly.*) You think I'll do?

YVONNE. Well—you're far better than others I see.

ROUSSEL. That's because I'm the only one here.

YVONNE. (*Teasing.*) That's a good reason. (*Changing tone.*) Do you want me to tell you that you're charming? Attractive? Appealing?

ROUSSEL. Yes.

YVONNE. Very well, my charming, attractive, appealing, *persistent* man. (ROUSSEL *kisses her hand, then sits* L. *of table.*)

ROUSSEL. I also write poetry.

YVONNE. Oh, yes. And that's unusual for a doctor. You know how the heart of a woman melts when she hears poetry.

ROUSSEL. (*Very pleased, then with affected modesty.*) You're too generous. I wouldn't call my poems great.

YVONNE. No?

ROUSSEL. (*Quickly, with undisguised vanity.*) But, they're not too bad. Others might call them great. (*Earnestly.*) Have you read my volume of verse yet? The one called "Heart-Drops"?

YVONNE. Not yet—my husband took it to read. (*Changing her tone.*) You know, it's not astonishing that you should have a place in my heart—a very special little corner.

ROUSSEL. Little Jack Horner sat in his corner—

YVONNE. (*Interrupting.*) I'm being sickeningly serious and you're being flippant.

ROUSSEL. Pardon me. Continue, my dear. You were saying that I have a place in your heart.

YVONNE. There is room for all our affections in the heart. And the heart is so big that the affection for one person need not conflict with affection for another.

ROUSSEL. Don't you think it could get over-crowded?

YVONNE. (*Rising, speaks squarely to* ROUSSEL.) No. The woman can order her heart—but the wife cannot order the woman—because the wife belongs only to her husband. (*She goes down* R.)

ROUSSEL. Her husband! Must you always come back to him?

YVONNE. Don't speak ill of him—he's your friend.

ROUSSEL. (*Rising.*) Of course, he's my friend. More than that—he trusts me.

YVONNE. (*With a shake of the head and a significant rictus.*) And this is the way you return his friendship?

ROUSSEL. I love *him*— I love you on the side, that's all.

YVONNE. And would you allow me to deceive him?

ROUSSEL. That's his concern, not mine.

YVONNE. (*Very straightforward.*) Listen to me, Roussel—when people are married, they swear fidelity to each other.

ROUSSEL. (*Bantering.*) Only because the words are in the marriage ceremony.

YVONNE. No matter. Until I have proof that my husband is deceiving me, I'll be faithful to him.

ROUSSEL. (*With eloquence.*) As the French general said to the English general: "Messieurs, fire the first shot." (*Thrusts his chest out, arms back.*)

YVONNE. Exactly. If I had proof—even this very day —that my husband was unfaithful, I swear I would run to you and say: "Roussel, avenge me." (*She goes close to him.*)

ROUSSEL. (*Carried away, tries to embrace her.*) Ah, Yvonne! Really?

YVONNE. (*Cutting short his elation.*) But that's an impossible assumption. (*She goes to fireplace, looks in mirror.*)

Roussel. (*Leaning on table, facing audience.*) You believe that? What does he love? Boating and hunting. Those are the only athletic exercises he allows himself.

Yvonne. I know that very well.

Roussel. (*Treacherously.*) Oh, there are many husbands who say they love to hunt. Do you know why? Because hunting offers a perfect excuse to go on the loose. They say: "I'm going hunting, darling." Once outside—oh, la, la—you should see.

Yvonne. But not my husband.

Roussel. Maybe not. Oh, I've thought about it, and I've asked myself: Could it be that my friend Chandel—?" But then I tell myself: "No." To tell you the truth, when he returns from a hunt, he looks like—well—a hunter returning from a hunt—nothing more.

Yvonne. You see.

Roussel. (*Slyly.*) But there are other little indications that puzzle me sometimes.

Yvonne. What little indications? (*She goes to him.*)

Roussel. (*Leaving the table, trying to be casual.*) Oh, I don't know. (*Then to the attack.*) For example—the other day he brought you a basket full of hares and rabbits which he said he had shot on his hunt.

Yvonne. Well?

Roussel. It's a known fact— (*Emphasizing each word.*) that where there are rabbits, there are no hares—and where there are hares, there are no rabbits.

Yvonne. (*Nervously.*) How do you know that?

Roussel. I studied Zoology. There is only one place where those two rodents are found together.

Yvonne. Well—perhaps that's where he went to find them.

Roussel. Exactly! The place I'm speaking of is the butcher's shop. (*He goes* L.)

Yvonne. (*Going to him.*) That's too much! Couldn't you have told me that sooner—you who pretend to be my friend? You left me here to sleep in blissful ignorance. I'm going to have an explanation from Chandel. (*She starts to door*, L.)

ROUSSEL. (*Following her.*) No! No! No! Don't do that! Listen to me, Yvonne—I told you at first that I didn't suspect your husband. I wouldn't have told you all that rubbish if I hadn't been convinced of his innocence.

YVONNE. You say that now! But I want to hear what he says about it. Here comes my husband. (CHANDEL *is heard singing offstage, "A Hunting We Will Go."*)

ROUSSEL. Yvonne—don't tell him what I said—it's madness. I'm leaving! (*He starts out as* CHANDEL *enters from* L.)

CHANDEL. (*By his door.*) Are you leaving?

ROUSSEL. (*Very embarrassed.*) No—yes. How are you?

CHANDEL. (*Going a little to rear.*) How am I? But you saw me before.

ROUSSEL. Did I? Well—I'll be off.

CHANDEL. It looks like rain. Do you want my umbrella?

ROUSSEL. Certainly not! I have my cane. (*He takes his cane which is near the door, and goes out.*)

CHANDEL. Did someone hit him with a hammer? What got into him? (*Seeing* YVONNE *nervously creasing a paper at desk.*) And you, too? What's wrong? What's been going on between you two?

YVONNE. (*Acidly.*) I just had a lesson in Zoology that taught me a great deal.

CHANDEL. Really? What did you learn?

YVONNE. What every young married woman should know but is afraid to ask.

CHANDEL. What could that be?

YVONNE. (*Going toward him.*) I learned that where there are rabbits there are no hares, and where there are hares there are no rabbits.

CHANDEL. (*Very sarcastic.*) A very interesting thing to know!

YVONNE. More than you think. If you had known it,

you probably wouldn't have brought me a basket of hares and rabbits from your last hunting expedition.

CHANDEL. Oh—I see—the lesson concerns me.

YVONNE. And me. I thought hares and rabbits were in the same family because they look alike. Happily, Roussel informed me that I was wrong.

CHANDEL. Roussel told you all this?

YVONNE. (*Passing to* L.) A slip of the tongue—with no malice intended.

CHANDEL. He's an idiot.

YVONNE. An idiot is he, because he set me straight on my husband's conduct?

CHANDEL. No—but because his Zoology lesson is going to worry you, and there is no reason for it.

YVONNE. Prove to me that there is no reason—prove it if you can.

CHANDEL. (*Nonchalantly.*) That's easy.

YVONNE. Well—prove it! (*She sits at table,* L.)

CHANDEL. (*Sitting at table facing her.*) Well—uh— your friend, Madame Chardet, has quarrelled with Madame Fontenac, I believe.

YVONNE. (*Imperative.*) Don't change the subject!

CHANDEL. (*Very calm.*) I'm not. Madame Chardet quarrelled with Madame Fontenac—yes or no?

YVONNE. (*Very dryly.*) Yes.

CHANDEL. Consequently, they don't see each other.

YVONNE. (*Impatiently.*) Naturally.

CHANDEL. When you want to see them—what do you do?

YVONNE. I go to their homes.

CHANDEL. Their homes—plural.

YVONNE. (*On edge.*) Get back to your rabbits.

CHANDEL. I've never left them. So you find Madame Chardet where she lives, and you find Madame Fontenac where she lives. True?

YVONNE. What about it?

CHANDEL. What about it? The rabbits are Madame Chardet—and the hares are Madame Fontenac.

YVONNE. (*Not comprehending.*) What do you mean—
the rabbits are Madame Chardet—?

CHANDEL. I mean—that when I want to hunt rabbits,
I go where the rabbits live, and when I want to hunt
hares, I go where the hares live. If both end up in the
same basket, it isn't because they're on speaking terms.
(*Opens eyes wide, amazed at his ability as a liar.*)

YVONNE. Oh—I understand now. Rabbits—Madame
Chardet—hares—Madame Fontenac.

CHANDEL. Of course.

YVONNE. Oh, my dear, I was wrong to suspect you.
(*Rises, goes behind* CHANDEL, *puts her hands on his
shoulders.*)

CHANDEL. Yes! You were very foolish. (*He kisses her
hand.*) To think that you would suspect your husband.

YVONNE. Oh!

CHANDEL. (*With comic indignation.*) You believe
others but you don't believe your own husband.

YVONNE. (*Goes around* R. *of table and crosses to* L.)
It was all Roussel's fault—he got me upset with his rabbits and hares.

CHANDEL. Wasn't I right to call him an idiot? Now I
know why he left in such a disturbed state. He even forgot his hat. (*Points to hat.*)

YVONNE. He lost his head.

CHANDEL. Then he didn't need his hat. (*Goes to*
YVONNE.) Promise me—no more foolish ideas. Kiss me.
(*She kisses him.*) Now come with me to choose my clothes
for today. (*A bell rings.*)

YVONNE. That must be Roussel.

CHANDEL. He probably found his head, and noticed
that his hat wasn't on it. (ROUSSEL, *embarrassed, enters
and goes* R. *of table.*)

ROUSSEL. It's me. I forgot my hat.

CHANDEL. I was just telling Yvonne that. Listen to me,
my friend, I have a score to settle with you. What have
you been telling my wife?

ROUSSEL. Me?

CHANDEL. Yes—you and your rabbits and hares. Were you trying to convince her that my hunting trips are a hoax?

ROUSSEL. (*Floundering.*) Oh, I said—what I said was —well, on the contrary, I didn't say—I mean—what I mean is—if you had seen her face—you would know— I mean—she wouldn't believe such things—besides, I was defending you.

CHANDEL. Very kind of you.

YVONNE. Calm down, Roussel—my husband explained everything.

ROUSSEL. (*Muddled, he addresses one, then the other.*) I'm glad to hear that—you see—because, you see— I was telling you—oh, she was imagining things about the rabbits and hares—but I said to you: "What does that prove, rabbits and hares?"—but you know women—you see—

YVONNE. It's very simple: the rabbits were Madame Chardet.

ROUSSEL. Of course.

YVONNE. And the hares were Madame Fontenac.

ROUSSEL. (*Mechanically, in a daze.*) It's clear—the hares were Madame——

YVONNE. Fontenac.

ROUSSEL. Fontenac. And the rabbits were Madame—

YVONNE. Chardet.

ROUSSEL. Of course! Nothing could be simpler. I'm glad I was here to learn that.

CHANDEL. Then all's well. We're not angry with you. But in the future, please don't upset my household with your vast knowledge.

ROUSSEL. You know, if I could have foreseen—

YVONNE. (*To* CHANDEL.) You're not angry with *me*, are you?

CHANDEL. Angry with you, my darling? (*Takes her in his arms, holds her close, kisses her.*) There! That's how angry I am. (*Kisses her again.* ROUSSEL, *who can't stand the sight, assumes a strange attitude, like a frozen heap.*

CHANDEL *looks up and notices him.*) Roussel—are you posing for "the Dying Swan"? (ROUSSEL *quickly regains his composure as* BABETTE *enters from rear.*)

BABETTE. The tailor has brought you some clothing, Monsieur.

CHANDEL. Oh, yes—have him go to my bedroom.

BABETTE. Yes, Monsieur. (*She starts to leave but* CHANDEL *calls her back.*)

CHANDEL. Oh, Babette—have they returned my gun?

BABETTE. Yes, Monsieur. (*She exits.*)

CHANDEL. You're now going to see my new clothes. I have a new tailor—he's very fashionable. He's the one who dresses my nephew Pierre.

ROUSSEL. The fact is that your nephew Pierre pays more attention to his clothes than to the institution that will give him his degree.

CHANDEL. (*With indulgent good humor.*) That's because his body is much larger than his head.

ROUSSEL. You're right. I never thought of that.

YVONNE. Let's go see your new clothes. (*She goes out* L., *taking cartridge pouch with her.*)

CHANDEL. (*Following her.*) Wait here, Roussel. If you get bored—read a book.

ROUSSEL. I will.

CHANDEL. (*Coming back to* ROUSSEL.) By the way— I want to thank you for the volume of verse. What was the title? "Heart-Burn," wasn't it?

ROUSSEL. (*Hurt.*) Heart-Drops.

CHANDEL. That's right—I knew it had heart. I haven't had the opportunity of reading it yet, but I left it in this room so that visitors may have a look at it.

ROUSSEL. Thank you. (CHANDEL *goes out.*) Heart-burn! That's the abuse a poet must take. And who is he to judge? I wonder where he put my book. (*Looks around, finally finds book under desk leg.*) My book! A prop for a wobbly desk! And to think that I paid a fortune to get this published. I'll speak to Chandel about this. (*Opens book and looks at it fondly.*) "Heart-Drops—

sonnets and other poems by Gustave Roussel, pediatri-
cian." (*Puts book down and starts thinking.*) Hares, rabbits—Madame Chardet—Madame Fontenac— (*Rises,
faces audience.*) What the devil was she talking about?
Madame Chardet doesn't look like a rabbit—and Madame
Fontenac—well—perhaps she does. But there must be
more to it than that. Rabbits—hares— (*He paces, gives
a gesture of resignation, sits at desk and picks up his book
again as* CHANDEL *enters from* L.)

CHANDEL. Well—what do you think of these trousers?

ROUSSEL. (*With contemptuous air, not even looking
up.*) Very nice—very nice.

CHANDEL. They should be. Pierre had a pair made exactly like them.

ROUSSEL. By the way, I want to thank you for the way
you displayed my book.

CHANDEL. (*Crossing to fireplace.*) You found it?

ROUSSEL. Yes. Under the leg of the desk.

CHANDEL. Good! That's where I put it. It isn't always
easy to put poetry to practical use, you know.

ROUSSEL. I didn't write it to be used as a prop. And
to think that I took the trouble to dedicate one of my
best poems to you. (*He goes by table, facing fireplace.*)

CHANDEL. You dedicated a poem to me?

ROUSSEL. If you had opened the book, you would have
seen it. It's called "Despair."

CHANDEL. "Despair?" And dedicated to me?

ROUSSEL. (*Holds up the book to him.*) See! "To my
friend, Chandel—Despair."

CHANDEL. Thanks—that cheers me up.

ROUSSEL. (*Reading, and moving around with eloquent
gestures.*)
"Believe me, friend, this life is strange,
 So full of unpredicted change;
 Today you're gay and full of mirth,
 Tomorrow, six feet under earth."

CHANDEL. That's a very gay poem.

ROUSSEL. Sh! (*Reading.*)
"But when you're gone forever more,
  My heart will be so sad and sore;
  Where will I be without you, friend?
  A lonely wanderer till the end."
CHANDEL. Enough! Your poem is making me ill.
ROUSSEL. But you haven't heard the conclusion. (*Reading.*)
"But we shall meet again one day,
  In some fair land so far away.
  Will it be heaven? Who can tell?
  For you, my friend, I'd go to hell."

(CHANDEL *puts his arm on* ROUSSEL'S *shoulder.*)

CHANDEL. Now that we have been joyfully united in hell, you must excuse me. My tailor is still here. (*Starts out, turns back.*) My friend, take my advice—devote all your time to the practice of medicine. (*He exits,* L.)
ROUSSEL. Some people have no love for literature. (*He leans on table, admiring his book, facing audience. A moment, and* PIERRE *enters. He wears trousers like* CHANDEL'S.)
PIERRE. (*Goes to* ROUSSEL, *who has not seen him, puts his hand on his shoulder.*) Doctor Roussel—how are you?
ROUSSEL. Pierre! It's good to see you. Are you on vacation?
PIERRE. (*Putting hat on table.*) Yes—for one day. My degree-grinder is shut down.
ROUSSEL. What?
PIERRE. I said "my degree-grinder is shut down." My school is having a holiday.
ROUSSEL. You invent your own language. In my time we would have said "the rat-trap is unhinged," that's all.
PIERRE. (*Pirouetting to gain extreme* R.) A language must evolve in order to flourish. (*Back to* ROUSSEL.) Tell me—is my uncle about?
ROUSSEL. Yes—in the next room. He was just trying on your trousers.

Pierre. What? *My* trousers?

Roussel. They're exactly like those you're wearing.

Pierre. (*Like a spoiled child.*) He's copying me, is he? That's a bore!

Roussel. (*Mimicking his tone.*) Yes, it's a bore! You'll find him with his tailor if you want to see him.

Pierre. The truth is, I want to see him, but I'm not overly anxious.

Roussel. No?

Pierre. I came to ask him for a loan, you see.

Roussel. Yes, I see.

Pierre. I already owe him some money—that's the rub. Six hundred francs.

Roussel. (*Takes* Pierre *by ear and moves him downstage.*) Ah, ha, my boy—are you keeping a girl?

Pierre. (*Raising his head, almost in bass voice.*) Yes!

Roussel. I can't believe it. What's she like? (Pierre *gives a drawn-out whistle.* Roussel *laughs.*)

Pierre. Oh, she's a gem—young and fresh—and she hasn't rolled around.

Roussel. You don't say?

Pierre. I don't count the old fellow. She calls him the monkey. She said to me: "If the monkey ever shows up, hide in the closet." He probably thinks he's the only one. Isn't that a laugh? But he doesn't bother me.

Roussel. (*Affecting.*) Where did you meet this marvelous creature?

Pierre. (*With a sublime look.*) I met this angel at the pawn shop.

Roussel. The pawn shop?

Pierre. Yes. She was pawning the family jewels, and I was getting rid of my watch. It was love at first sight.

Roussel. Very touching—Romeo and Juliet of the Pawn Shop.

Pierre. That same day she gave me the key to her apartment and to her heart. Since then, I see her every Sunday—except last Sunday when I was restricted. But since I have a holiday, I'll see her tonight. Oh, the devil!

I wrote a telegram to tell her I was coming tonight but I forgot to send it. (*He looks through his pockets.*) She'll be happy to see me after two weeks of abstinence. Of course, there's the old fellow, but you know, he— (*Flaps his hand loosely, laughs, and then looks at a paper he has just found in his pocket.*)

ROUSSEL. Did you find it?

PIERRE. No—this is not it. This is a guarantee I brought for my uncle in case he breaks down and lends me five hundred francs.

ROUSSEL. So, you give guarantees?

PIERRE. (*With comic importance.*) Yes—a little paper that I dashed off. (*Hands it to* ROUSSEL.)

ROUSSEL. (*Reading.*) "On the day of my majority, I will pay to my Uncle Chandel the sum of five hundred francs." (*Looks up.*) That's a guarantee, all right.

PIERRE. (*Takes paper and puts it in his pocket.*) That paper is worth money. (*Finds another paper in his pocket.*) Here's my telegram. I'll have Babette send it. (*He pulls the bell-cord, then to* ROUSSEL, *with hesitation.*) I was just thinking—to help me avoid this ordeal with my uncle, would it put you out to lend me the five hundred?

ROUSSEL. No, it wouldn't put me out.

PIERRE. (*Pausing, shakes his head.*) I could give you my guarantee.

ROUSSEL. I know—but I wouldn't think of depriving your uncle of the pleasure. (*He crosses to extreme* L.)

PIERRE. Well—it was just a routine question.

BABETTE. (*Entering from rear, speaks to* ROUSSEL.) Did you ring, Monsieur?

ROUSSEL. No—it was Pierre. (*He thumbs through his book on the desk.*)

PIERRE. Babette—will you send this telegram for me? (*Hands her the paper.*)

BABETTE. A telegram? (*Reading.*) "Mademoiselle Fifi Limande, thirty-five, Avenue Gambetta."

PIERRE. I asked you to send it, not read it.

BABETTE. Very well, Monsieur.

PIERRE. Here are two francs. (*With a lordly air.*) You may keep the change.

BABETTE. (*Sarcastic.*) You're too generous, Monsieur. I'll buy an evening-gown. (*She exits.*)

ROUSSEL. (*Goes to* PIERRE *and then to* R.) Your uncle is coming. You can make your request.

PIERRE. Already? I'm getting nervous. (CHANDEL *and* YVONNE *enter.*)

CHANDEL. I'm ready.

YVONNE. Pierre!

(ROUSSEL *is by fireplace,* PIERRE *near him,* YVONNE *above table,* CHANDEL *at* L.)

PIERRE. (*Crossing to* L.) Bonjour, my dear aunt—bonjour, my dear uncle. It's true—you do have on my trousers. (*Hold his leg up next to* CHANDEL'S.)

CHANDEL. (*Also extending his leg.*) Yes, yes, my boy— we copy each other. (PIERRE, *to win his uncle's good-will, bends down to examine his uncle's trousers as a tailor would. He runs his hand down the crease and holds the cuff of trousers.*) I must send a telegram. (*He starts to move but almost falls over because of* PIERRE.) Watch what you're doing. (*Goes to desk, finds it wobbly, takes* ROUSSEL'S *book and starts to put it under leg.*)

ROUSSEL. (*Indignant.*) Oh, no, you don't, my friend. Not my book! Use Victor Hugo for that.

CHANDEL. Never mind the desk. (*He sits at desk.*) What time is it?

ROUSSEL. I have five after five.

YVONNE. I have ten after five.

CHANDEL. (*To* PIERRE.) And you, Pierre?

PIERRE. (*Taking an old nickel-plated watch from his pocket.*) I have nine-thirty.

CHANDEL. You must not be running.

PIERRE. (*Laughing.*) I don't think so. (*Slowly, scratching his head, as if trying to think what to do, he goes* R., *above table.*)

CHANDEL. (*Begins to write.*) I have no time to lose if I expect to catch the six o'clock train.

YVONNE. (*Goes to* CHANDEL.) Are you wiring Castillo?

CHANDEL. (*Quickly turning over the paper.*) Yes—Castillo—to tell him what time to meet me at the station. Will you please tell Babette to take my bag and my gun down?

YVONNE. Yes, my dear husband. (*She exits, rear.*)

CHANDEL. (*Writing.*) "Madame Castillo, thirty-five Avenue Gambetta."

ROUSSEL. (*Near* PIERRE *by fireplace.*) Aren't you going to ask him?

PIERRE. When he finishes writing.

CHANDEL. (*Writing.*) "I'll be there at seven o'clock—Zizi." (*As* CHANDEL *folds the paper and puts it in his pocket,* PIERRE *crosses towards him.*)

PIERRE. Uncle!

CHANDEL. (*Rising, distractedly.*) Let's see—do I have enough money? (*Takes wad of bills from his pocket.*)

ROUSSEL. (*Low, to* PIERRE.) Courage—he has it in his hand.

PIERRE. (*After a violent effort.*) Uncle, since you have so many one hundred franc notes—could you give me five?

CHANDEL. Not one franc, my nephew. You already owe me six hundred—that's sufficient.

PIERRE. Just a moment! I don't understand why you speak to me in that way. I'm not asking you for a loan. I see a large number of one hundred franc notes in your hand. I simply want you to give me five in exchange for a very good note for five hundred francs.

CHANDEL. Oh—you want change? Why didn't you say so? (*While he counts, a bill falls without his seeing it.* PIERRE *quickly catches it in his hat and puts his hat on his head.*) One—two—three—four—five—there you are —five hundred francs.

PIERRE. And here's your note for five hundred. (*Takes*

his "guarantee" from pocket and hands it to CHANDEL, *then goes behind table.*)

CHANDEL. What's this? (*Reading.*) "On the day of my majority—"

PIERRE. Tit for tat.

CHANDEL. (*Runs after* PIERRE.) Oh, no! None of that! Give me back my five hundred francs.

PIERRE. (*Making half circles around table,* R. *to* L., *then* L. *to* R., *always keeping table between them.*) You accepted it, uncle. My note is now in circulation.

CHANDEL. Not at all—not at all.

PIERRE. Au revoir, uncle—and many thanks. (*He runs out.*)

CHANDEL. (*Running to door.*) Pierre! Come back here, you crook!

ROUSSEL. (*Laughing.*) My friend, I think the best thing you can do is to endorse his note.

YVONNE. (*Entering at rear with* CHANDEL'S *hunting hat.*) What happened? Pierre ran out as if the house were on fire.

CHANDEL. He swindled me out of five hundred francs—that's what happened.

YVONNE. (*Laughing.*) No!

ROUSSEL. But he left you something of equal value.

CHANDEL. Equal value? If I sold it to you for three francs, I would be guilty of theft. But I'll catch him.

YVONNE. I'm not trying to send you away, but if you want to catch the six-o'clock train— (*She puts the hat on* CHANDEL'S *head.*)

CHANDEL. You're right. (*Door bell rings.*)

YVONNE. Some one rang. (BABETTE *enters from* R.)

BABETTE. Monsieur Chandel, there's a gentleman in the salon who wishes to speak to you.

CHANDEL. I don't have much time. Who is he?

BABETTE. He didn't tell me his name.

CHANDEL. Too bad. You talk to him, Yvonne—I must run. Babette, did you take down my bag and my gun?

BABETTE. Yes, Monsieur. (*She goes into door,* R.)

CHANDEL. Au revoir, my little Yvonne.

YVONNE. Au revoir, my dear. Be careful not to have an accident. (*They kiss.* ROUSSEL, *disgusted, sneers.*)

CHANDEL. Are you coming down with me, Roussel?

ROUSSEL. Yes, I'll walk downstairs with you. (*He goes to pick up hat.*)

CHANDEL. (*At door.*) Hurry! Yvonne, when the clock strikes seven, you can say to yourself: "My husband is on the lands of his friend Castillo." (*He dashes out.*)

ROUSSEL. (*Going as far as door, then turning to* YVONNE.) Well, Yvonne?

YVONNE. What?

ROUSSEL. You know very well "what."

YVONNE. No!

ROUSSEL. (*With a look of resignation.*) Oh! (*He exits.*)

BABETTE. (*Entering from* R.) Shall I have the gentleman come in now?

YVONNE. Yes—yes—show him in.

BABETTE. (*Opens door,* R., *and announces.*) Monsieur Castillo.

YVONNE. Who? Castillo?

(CASTILLO, *a very amiable Latin with an accent, enters, goes* R. *of table. The extent of his accent is up to the director, but certain mispronunciations are indicated in the script.*)

CASTILLO. Madame, I am happy to see you. How is Monsieur Chandel? Is he here?

YVONNE. (L., *below table.*) No, he's not here. Did you perhaps wish to speak to him? (*She is worried, but tries to hide it.*)

CASTILLO. Yes, Madame. It is a very long time since I have seen him.

YVONNE. It is? (*She moves in direction of table.*)

CASTILLO. I wish to speak with him on a private matter. I can confide in you? (YVONNE, *nervous but contained, motions him to sit. She sits also, at* L., *he at* R.

CASTILLO *puts his hat and cane on table.*) You know that I live separate from my wife, and that I want very much to have a divorce.

YVONNE. (*More concerned about other matters.*) Yes, I understand, but—

CASTILLO. (*Cutting her words.*) I did not have the grounds for divorce. But now, I came to tell my friend that I have grounds. Oh, yes, very good grounds—my wife has a lover. And tonight, I intend to surprise my wife with him. She has a lover, Madame, and I know it—yes, she has a lover.

YVONNE. (*Has not heard a word he said, occupied as she is with all the questions in her mind.*) That's very nice—that's very nice.

CASTILLO. His name is Monsieur Zizi.

YVONNE. My compliments, my compliments. You were saying that you have not seen my husband for a long time.

CASTILLO. A very long time.

YVONNE. But you must see him when you go hunting, don't you?

CASTILLO. Hunt? I never hunt.

YVONNE. You never hunt?

CASTILLO. Never in my life.

YVONNE. He doesn't hunt! (*She is literally suffocating. She leaps up and utters a series of raucous cries which cause* CASTILLO *to jump backwards.*) Ah! Ah! Ah! Ah! Ah!

CASTILLO. (*Composing himself.*) What is it?

YVONNE. (*Seeming to address* CASTILLO, *but really oblivious of him.*) Liar! Cheat! Wretch!

CASTILLO. (*Shocked.*) But, Madame—what did I say?

YVONNE. (*Marching on* CASTILLO.) Are you going to tell me now that you go hunting? (*She moves to rear,* L.)

CASTILLO. (*Following her.*) Me? No—on the contrary.

YVONNE. (*Opening rear door as if* CHANDEL *were there.*) You play games with me! You make a fool of me! You treat me like a moron!

CASTILLO. Está loca en la cabeza! (*He goes quickly downstage.*)

YVONNE. (*Descending on him, causing him to go* L.) The mask has fallen at last, and you appear in all the blackness of your soul. (*She is above table at* L.)

CASTILLO. (*He approaches table, puts hands on it, trying to soothe her.*) Señora—

YVONNE. (*Kicking him in the shin.*) Leave me alone!

CASTILLO. Oh! Tenga cuidado, que puede matarme! (*Recoils on one leg, rubbing his shin.*)

YVONNE. Now I know what I wanted to know. I suspected it.

CASTILLO. Madame—your nerves—

YVONNE. Ridicule me, will you? (*She picks up* CASTILLO'S *cane and menaces him with it.*) We'll see who has the last laugh. When I think that I was a blind fool. (*She sits* L. *of table.*)

CASTILLO. (*Approaching her cautiously.*) Yes, Madame, yes.

YVONNE. I was calm! I was happy! I was contented! (*On each exclamation she pounds* CASTILLO'S *hat.*)

CASTILLO. Mi sombrero, Señora—my hat!

YVONNE. Take your hat! (*She throws the hat at him with vigor.*) How stupid can a woman be? (*She strikes the table with the cane.*) But now it's my turn! (*She rings the call-bell.*) I've been too good—but you know the law of retaliation. (*Turns sharply to* CASTILLO, *shrieking, tries to choke him.*) Do you know the law of retaliation?

CASTILLO. (*Really frightened.*) Sí Señora, sí—

YVONNE. This home doesn't satisfy you! Well, it doesn't satisfy me either. It's time for a change. First, I'll write to Roussel.

BABETTE. (*Entering from rear.*) Did Madame ring?

YVONNE. Yes! Pack my bag! I'm going to spend the night with my aunt—in the country. Be quick about it. (*She goes down* L.)

BABETTE. (*Low, to* CASTILLO.) What's the matter with her?

CASTILLO. She's seek—very seek. (BABETTE *exits.*)

YVONNE. I'll have my revenge—sweet revenge! Lying, cheating, sneaking monster! (*In anger, she breaks* CASTILLO'S *cane, throws it at him furiously, and storms out* R.)

CASTILLO. (*In a pitiful voice, picking up pieces of his cane.*) My steek! (*Blackout.*)

CURTAIN

END OF ACT ONE

NOTE: If facilities exist for a quick change of sets between Act One and Act Two, the intermission at this point can be eliminated. During the change, CHANDEL crosses in front of curtain, carrying his bag and gun-case, and singing A HUNTING WE WILL GO as he crosses.

ACT TWO

The bachelor apartment of ROUSSEL. *Elegant, but gaudy furnishings. Down* R., *an upright piano against the wall. The piano is open, and a piece of music is on the stand. Round, swivel-type stool. There are curios on the piano. At* R., *above piano, a door which opens into the room. It has a workable lock. At rear,* R., *an elegant alcove draped with bright valance and curtains of silk. The curtains open with a pull-cord. In alcove is a bed with head at* R. *Near bed, a night-stand with candlestick. Before the bed is a bear-skin rug. At rear,* L. *of bed, double French window, full-length, with Venetian blinds. It has a valance and curtains matching the alcove. The window opens on a balcony with a view of the street by moonlight. The balcony railing extends out of sight in both di-rections. Up* L., *a door. Down* L., *a wall-papered door to a closet. Between the two* L. *doors is a fire-place with fire. On the mantel, matches, candle, hand mirror, two candelabrums, and a statuette. Above fireplace, an artistic oval mirror. Side of door,* R., *a bell-cord. About a yard from fireplace, facing front, is a small sofa with several cushions on it. On the* R. *side, a yard from the piano, a table with two covers, a chair on each side. On the table, a small lamp. Also two shrimp cocktails, covered dishes, a butter dish, glasses, bottle of Bordeaux wine in a basket. Ad lib, throughout room, are curios, pic-tures, and other art objects.*

At rise of curtain, MADAME LATOUR, *an old aristocrat, is tidying the room. She is dressed in eccentric fashion. She is energetically spraying the window curtains with an atomizer.*

LATOUR. Enough for the curtains. Now for the sofa. That's generally where the action starts. It's very important. Final victory often depends on the outcome of the first skirmish. Double ration for the sofa. (*She sprays the sofa well.*) You see, I spray strategically. (*Goes over to bed, opens the curtains.*) The bed is just a matter of form. If they get this far, the war is over. One squirt for reconstruction. (*A quick spray on bed, then draws curtains, goes* L., *by sofa.*) I hope that Doctor Roussel, the new tenant, is satisfied. (*Hold up spray bottle.*) I've used up almost sixteen francs worth of Imperial Russian. But he won't mind. Oh, I love men who don't care about expense. There's nothing too good for a woman who is loved. We're the favored sex. (*She sprays herself well with the atomizer.*) Too bad that I, the Countess de Latour, couldn't have met a man like this instead of a circus performer. My husband wouldn't have caught me, and I wouldn't be a concierge today. (*She sits on sofa, then stretches out on it.*) But—what the hell—that was a long time ago. Happy hours—some of them. Oh, this perfume intoxicates me. I feel much too sensuous for a concierge. But what good will it do me? (*Sighs deeply, sits up.*) But maybe it's true what the proverb says: "There's no woman so high, but has her hour with the devil." Why doesn't the devil ever come to see me?

CHANDEL. (*Outside door,* R.) Madame Latour!

LATOUR. Maybe that's the devil! (*She leaps up and goes toward the door.*)

CHANDEL. (*Outside.*) Madame Latour!

LATOUR. Who's calling me?

CHANDEL. It's Monsieur Zizi.

LATOUR. Oh—Monsieur Zizi. (*She opens door to admit him.*)

CHANDEL. I've been looking for you for fifteen minutes, Madame Latour. What smells in here? Is there a cat?

LATOUR. I'll have you know this is Imperial Russian Toilet Water. (*She sprays some for him to smell.*)

CHANDEL. Phew! You could knock a man down with

that. (*To the point.*) Madame Latour, I've been ringing and ringing the door across the hall. Madame Castillo isn't at home.

LATOUR. (*With a desolate air.*) No, Monsieur.

CHANDEL. But I sent her a message. Didn't she get it?

LATOUR. Yes, Monsieur. Madame Castillo told me that her uncle—her Uncle Zizi—

CHANDEL. That's me.

LATOUR. Her uncle Zizi was arriving today. She said that if she had known earlier, she would have been able to meet you, but she had made plans that could not be changed. She asked me to give you the key to her apartment, and to tell you to wait for her. (*She hands* CHANDEL *a key.*)

CHANDEL. Thank you, but it would have been better if she stayed here.

LATOUR. She won't be gone long, Monsieur. Tell me, Monsieur Zizi—why do you always bring your gun?

CHANDEL. Gun? (*Forgetting he was holding it.*) Oh, yes—my gun. Well—ugh—I love to hunt. You never know when you might run across a wild boar, or a panther, or a—

LATOUR. In Paris?

CHANDEL. Paris? Did you think I lived in Paris? I don't live in Paris. I live in the country.

LATOUR. In the country?

CHANDEL. Yes—in the middle of a forest. Sometimes, when I walk to the railway station, I see aminals, and then— (*Holds up gun case as if to fire towards window.*) Bang! Bang! (*Laughs heartily.*) Oh, I love to hunt.

LATOUR. (*Joining in the laughter.*) Oh, you're a happy hunter.

CHANDEL. (*Slapping her on the shoulder.*) Yes—a happy hunter. (*Then, looking around.*) You know—this is the first time I've seen this apartment. The little wench lives well.

LATOUR. Little wench? Oh—you mean Fifi Limande. She doesn't live here any longer. We asked her to leave.

CHANDEL. Really?

LATOUR. We can't have tenants like that. It gives the house a bad name. Do you know that she specialized in weaning college students? That reminds me—I must get the key she gave to her last young lover. Oh, Monsieur Zizi, she taught them all her tricks even before they got their degrees. (*Changing tone.*) Yes, I had to pull the cord on her. My patrician blood revolted. (*She strikes her chest with a noble gesture.*)

CHANDEL. You're a tyrant, Madame Latour.

LATOUR. For her sort—yes. Oh, I don't mind seeing decent women have their little affairs, but I have no respect for mercenary love. Happily, since she left, the house is above reproach—nothing but married people. And some of them are married to each other.

CHANDEL. Perfect! Water, lights, gas and married people on all floors. What about the new tenants in this apartment? Are they married?

LATOUR. He isn't—but I'm sure she is—judging from the mysterious way he spoke about her.

CHANDEL. Ah, ha—and what does he do?

LATOUR. He's a doctor.

CHANDEL. And she's probably one of his patients. Her poor husband will pay for his services. Well, Countess, I'm going to see if Madame Castillo has returned.

LATOUR. One moment, Monsieur. (*She opens the door slightly, very cautiously, and peeks out.*) Oh, Monsieur Zizi—it's the new tenants. They'll be angry because I allowed you to come in.

CHANDEL. Then I'll dash out.

LATOUR. (*Stopping him.*) No! No! They'll see you! Go in here. (*She takes his arm, guides him to closet door, down* L.) I'll tell them you're a relative of mine who has been helping me prepare the apartment. Quickly. (*She pushes him into the closet.*)

CHANDEL. (*Opening the door slightly.*) Good God— it smells of camphor in here.

LATOUR. It will preserve you. Wait until I come for

you. (*She closes door on him, just as* YVONNE *and* ROUS-
SEL *enter. She stands by closet.*)

ROUSSEL. Here it is—our little hide-away. Don't be
afraid—come in.

YVONNE. I don't dare stay.

ROUSSEL. (*Pulling her gently.*) What is there to be
afraid of?

YVONNE. (*Backing away, timidly.*) What if someone
sees me? (*Notices* LATOUR.) Oh—a woman.

ROUSSEL. What? Where? (*Turns to see* LATOUR.) Oh,
that? That's nothing at all.

LATOUR. Well!

ROUSSEL. (*Presenting, takes off his hat.*) Allow me to
introduce the Countess de Latour.

YVONNE. Madame— (*She curtsies.*)

ROUSSEL. She's my concierge.

YVONNE. (*Abashed.*) Your concierge?

LATOUR. Alas, yes, Madame—but a true aristocrat
nevertheless.

ROUSSEL. A Countess who ended up as a concierge—
she'll tell you all about it. Countess, you are at liberty to
leave us now. (*She starts to leave, but turns when she
hears a loud sneeze in the closet.*)

YVONNE. What's that noise? (*She tries to hide her face
with her veil.*)

ROUSSEL. (*Points to closet.*) Is someone in there? I
heard a sneeze.

LATOUR. (*Coming down a little, briskly.*) Yes, Monsieur—I had forgotten all about him. He's a relative of
mine who was helping me tidy the apartment.

ROUSSEL. But why is he in the closet?

LATOUR. You took us by surprise—and since I thought
that perhaps you would not care to have him see Madame,
I sent him in there. If you and Madame will go into the
next room for a moment, I'll dispose of him. (*She indicates door, up* L.)

ROUSSEL. Yes—do that—and quickly. (*Hands her a
coin.*) Give him this for his services.

LATOUR. Thank you, Monsieur—he'll be very grateful.

ROUSSEL. Come with me, my frightened fawn. (*He escorts* YVONNE *into room,* L.)

LATOUR. (*Opening closet door.*) Quickly, Monsieur Zizi —you can leave now. (CHANDEL *comes out.*)

CHANDEL. Thank you! I feel like I've been embalmed. (*After a thought.*) And this isn't the time for that. (*He starts off* R., *between table and sofa.*)

LATOUR. Please hurry. Here—this is for you—from the doctor. (*She hands him the coin.*)

CHANDEL. Oh, a tip. You keep it, Countess. No one must say I neglect my family.

LATOUR. Thank you, Monsieur. And now— (*She points to the door.*)

CHANDEL. (*Halfway to door, turns back.*) Tell me— are they in there? (*Points to door,* L.)

LATOUR. Who?

CHANDEL. The doctor and the adulteress.

LATOUR. Yes—they're in there. (*She laughs boisterously.*)

CHANDEL. (*Also laughing.*) That's funny.

LATOUR. (*Smothering her laughter, dead serious.*) What's so funny about it?

CHANDEL. The doctor and the patient! He'll probably double her husband's bill.

LATOUR. I feel sure it's the first time she's done this sort of thing.

CHANDEL. Really? (*A grand gesture.*) One more in the world! I salute her! (*He throws a kiss to the bedroom door.*) Faust and Marguerite—may Cupid protect you. Me—I'm Mephistopheles! (*A diabolical laugh.*) I go to Madame Castillo! (*He stalks out in theatrical fashion.*)

LATOUR. It's about time! (*She goes to open door,* L.) You may come out now. All clear! (*They come out.*) You have no more need of me, Monsieur?

ROUSSEL. (*Puts hat on fireplace mantel.*) No, thank you, Countess. (YVONNE, *behind sofa, takes off coat and hat while* ROUSSEL *and* LATOUR *speak.*)

LATOUR. Good-night, Monsieur and Madame.

ROUSSEL. Good-night to you, Countess. (*Takes off gloves, puts them on night-stand.*)

LATOUR. Me? What could be good about it for *me?* (*Shrugs shoulders and goes out.*)

ROUSSEL. (*Immediately going to* YVONNE, *rapturously.*) Yvonne! (*Starts to embrace her as* LATOUR, *like a jack-in-the-box, reappears.*)

LATOUR. (*Indicating bell-cord by door,* R.) If you need me—just ring. The bell goes to my quarters.

ROUSSEL. Yes, Countess—yes, Countess. Do like the bell, and go there too. (*Closes door on her and locks it.*) Yvonne! Alone at last! (*He holds her.*)

YVONNE. Roussel, is it really I? Am I really here—and in your arms?

ROUSSEL. (*Holding both her hands.*) I hardly believe it myself. I have to look at you—I have to feel you close to me. I need you. (*He starts to kiss her, but she puts her hand to her mouth.*) But I must—in order to know that it's really you—you, whom I have desired for so many days.

YVONNE. (*Slipping out of his embrace.*) Only the days?

ROUSSEL. And nights! Especially the nights.

YVONNE. Oh, Roussel—tell me that I'm not being foolish. (*She moves down a bit.*)

ROUSSEL. Foolish? In what way?

YVONNE. (*Sitting on sofa.*) In every way. Think—I'm still an honest woman and a faithful wife—but tomorrow—

ROUSSEL. (*With superb conviction.*) You will be tomorrow, too.

YVONNE. You don't mean that.

ROUSSEL. (*Very sincerely.*) You will be if you don't tell everybody in the world.

YVONNE. (*With instinctive terror.*) Oh! No!

ROUSSEL. What is honesty in a woman? It's public opinion. We simply keep our little affair to ourselves, and public opinion won't harm us.

Yvonne. How very moral!

Roussel. (*Vehemently.*) Are you going to tell me that propriety is anything more than a social convention? In what way are you not a proper woman simply because you give yourself to someone who loves you? Isn't it because society has said, "You will love no man but your husband—he is your legal lover?" (*Sits beside her on sofa, holding her hand.*) But natural law says: "Marriage is a union of two people who love each other." So, you see, the real husband is the lover—not the one the law gives you, but the one the heart chooses.

Yvonne. The second in command, you mean.

Roussel. That's right—a lieutenant. (*Rises, goes* R., *speaking half to himself.*) There always has to be someone to do the work. (*Back to* Yvonne.) But why are we discussing all this? Why are we arguing? We love each other, don't we? (*He takes her hand, but she rises, strolls to* R.) What does the rest matter? Have you already forgotten that letter you wrote to me in a surge of ecstasy?

Yvonne. (*Going down* R.) Ecstasy? I was mad as the devil.

Roussel. Mad ecstasy, then. But that letter opened the gates of Paradise to me. That letter—

Yvonne. Do you have it?

Roussel. Do I have it? I'll keep it forever—next to my heart. (*He strikes his heart with a noble gesture.*)

Yvonne. (*An air of misgiving, but full of coquetry.*) Oh, I would like very much to see it.

Roussel. Here it is. (*He digs the letter from his rear pocket.*)

Yvonne. (*Trying to hide a laugh.*) Did you say "next to your heart?"

Roussel. (*Slight pause, then with conviction.*) The heart is everywhere. Here is your letter—written in the sublime language that comes from here. (*Strikes his chest again.*)

Yvonne. Do you mean the heart this time?

Roussel. Of course. (*Reading.*) "My friend—

(*Touched, he kisses the letter.*) "My friend, I have only one word to say: at this time there is no longer any obstacle between us." (*Spoken.*) Eloquent and concise. (*Lyrically, charmed by his own words.*) Oh, the eloquence of its conciseness—and the conciseness of—

YVONNE. (*Taking his tone.*) Of its eloquence.

ROUSSEL. Yes! (*Reading.*) "Free from myself, I engage myself to you." (*Starts to fold the letter.*) That's what you wrote me.

YVONNE. But there's more—read it.

ROUSSEL. The rest is not important.

YVONNE. Yes it is. (*She reads over his shoulder.*) "Understand that I act as I do because *he* wishes it." (*Spoken.*) Did you hear that? "Because *he* wishes it."

ROUSSEL. I understand. It's a little concession to female pride.

YVONNE. (*Scornfully.*) Oh, do you think so?

ROUSSEL. (*Putting letter in his* side *trousers pocket.*) Do you honestly believe you could turn back after writing a letter like that? No! It's too late! Yvonne, doesn't everything around us invite us to love? (*His right arm around her waist, he gently pivots her so that they are back to audience.*) Smell the voluptuous perfume.

YVONNE. It smells like a Turkish harem.

ROUSSEL. (*Pivots her around, facing table.*) And do you see the table set for two? It's waiting for us—a supper for two souls bound by a tender passion.

YVONNE. (*Clapping her hands like a child.*) Oh— shrimp! My husband would love that.

ROUSSEL. He won't get any! Let him eat rabbit! Look at the soft light of the lamp. What mystery—what promise in its glow. (*Turns her toward the window.*) Even the moon has joined our party—the moon—that confidant of lovers. (*He opens the window.*)

YVONNE. (*Going closer to window.*) Oh, the moon is beautiful tonight. Look—you have a balcony.

ROUSSEL. Oh, yes. The balcony goes all around the

building. What a perfect setting for Romeo and Juliet.
That's us. Romeo and Juliet by the balcony.

YVONNE. Seen from the inside.

ROUSSEL. Romeo jumped over the balcony—oop la!
(*He leads her gently towards the bed, pulls cord to open
curtains.*) And here at last is—

YVONNE. (*Screaming.*) Oh!

ROUSSEL. What?

YVONNE. No! Not that! Not that! (*Really horrified,
she throws herself on sofa.*)

ROUSSEL. (*Goes to her, speaking very naturally.*) But,
it's the—

YVONNE. Yes! Yes! Oh, not that! Not that!

ROUSSEL. Why do you say "not that?" Oh, la, la—
don't be silly. (*Turns, speaks directly to audience.*) It's
like in surgery, one mustn't display one's instruments in
advance.

YVONNE. (*Face in hands.*) Oh, Roussel! (*She is sob-
bing.*)

ROUSSEL. What's the matter? You're crying. (YVONNE
rises.)

YVONNE. It seems that I'm getting married all over
again. (*Throws herself in his arms.*)

ROUSSEL. (*Height of bewilderment.*) Huh?

YVONNE. (*Still in his arms.*) It was like this on our
wedding night. *He* was near me—just as you are now.

ROUSSEL. (*Rather bored by it.*) Oh—him!

YVONNE. *He* was speaking tender words—as you have
been. And then—boom! (*She pushes* ROUSSEL *with both
hands so that he sprawls on the bed.*) The bed!

ROUSSEL. Don't tell me about him—it's disgusting.

YVONNE. Why did he have to deceive me? If he hadn't,
I wouldn't be here now.

ROUSSEL. (*Losing patience, he goes to her.*) Yvonne,
please stop talking about your husband—and if he is on
your mind, at least see him as he is today.

YVONNE. (*Passing to* R.) Don't talk about that.

ROUSSEL. I will talk about it, because, after all, his

conduct is shameful. Don't you realize that at this very moment he is whispering his words of love to another woman?

YVONNE. (*Crosses back to* ROUSSEL.) It's true. The scoundrel!

ROUSSEL. You have no reason to have scruples.

YVONNE. (*Raging.*) No! No scruples!

ROUSSEL. He has a mistress.

YVONNE. (*Her arms about his neck.*) And I have a lover!

ROUSSEL. At this very moment he is kissing her. (*He kisses* YVONNE.) He is holding her tightly in his arms.

YVONNE. Hold me! Hold me! (*He squeezes her tightly.*)

ROUSSEL. He's kissing her again.

YVONNE. Yes! (*Indicates her mouth.*) Here! Here! (*He kisses her.*)

ROUSSEL. Can you say his conduct is not shameful?

BOTH. (*Her indignation is sincere, his faked.*) Oh!

ROUSSEL. (*Brusquely.*) But wait! Now the woman is returning his kisses.

YVONNE. No!

ROUSSEL. Yes!

YVONNE. (*Exasperated.*) Yes—she's kissing him. (*She kisses* ROUSSEL *repeatedly on his face and neck.*)

ROUSSEL. I've waited all my life for this moment.

YVONNE. (*Exhausted, she sinks in chair at table.*) I'm thirsty.

ROUSSEL. (*Pacing to* L., *really touched.*) My love is thirsty! My love is thirsty! (*Returning to her.*) What would you like to drink?

YVONNE. (*Holding up a glass from table.*) Anything! Some champagne!

ROUSSEL. Good! Some champagne. (*Examines table.*) Where is the champagne? How could the Countess forget champagne? (*He strides to bell-cord by door,* R., *and pulls it.*) What could she have been thinking of?

YVONNE. Aren't you thirsty?

ROUSSEL. (*With giant steps, strides to her, crouches beside her amorously, his face against hers.*) I'm thirsty for you—thirsty for your love. (*Cuddling close, he declaims sensuously.*)
Your beauty warms me, it fills me with desire;
Your eyes devour me, they set me all on fire.
YVONNE. (*Eyes half-closed, she frames his head with her* L. *arm.*) Oh, yes—poetry! More verses, my poet.
ROUSSEL.
My heart burns with passion, just to hear your name;
The tender beauty of your smile sets my soul aflame.
YVONNE. (*Warmed by the verses.*) More! More!
ROUSSEL. (*With a pitiful air.*) That's all there is to that poem.
YVONNE. You mean you burned yourself out? Oh, Roussel, when you speak verse, I can't resist you.
ROUSSEL. (*Falling to his knees.*) She can't resist me! She can't resist me! (*With joy, he rolls his head in her two hands which are open on her knees. There is a knock at the door.* YVONNE *jumps up, causing* ROUSSEL *to sprawl on the floor. She goes* L.) Who is there?
LATOUR. (*Outside.*) It's me—the Countess Latour.
ROUSSEL. It's just the concierge. Come in! (*He goes to the door as* LATOUR *enters.*) Well, Countess, I'm disappointed in you. You prepare a charming supper for two, but you forget the champagne.
LATOUR. (*Very matter-of-fact.*) But, no, Monsieur— I didn't forget. You said to prepare something that *I* would like. (*A terrible face.*) Well—champagne turns my stomach.
ROUSSEL. But of course you have no difficulty in tolerating Bordeaux? (*He holds up the bottle of wine on the table.*)
LATOUR. Oh, no. But, Monsieur, if you desire champagne, you will find a bottle in the next room—on the top shelf of the cupboard, I believe.
ROUSSEL. I certainly do want it.
LATOUR. (*Starts to* L.) I'll get it for you.

ROUSSEL. No—the cupboard is too high for you. I'll go and look for it myself. You may keep Madame company.

LATOUR. (*Above sofa.*) Very well, Monsieur. (ROUSSEL *goes out* L., *throwing a kiss to* YVONNE *who sits on sofa.* LATOUR *closes window, then goes* R. *of sofa.*) That is what I call a gentleman.

YVONNE. You think so?

LATOUR. Certainly. With a man like that, a woman can permit herself a little folly.

YVONNE. For whom is that remark intended?

LATOUR. (*Quickly.*) It was a general observation. It applies to me, if you like. My greatest mistake was to favor a man who was beneath me in station.

YVONNE. Really?

LATOUR. (*With a bitter sigh.*) Ah, yes. It cost me my position in the world, Madame—because the world will forgive bad conduct, but never a scandal. I was disgraced in society. I was thrown out by my husband. You see the state I am in today.

YVONNE. Poor Countess. Who was this man?

LATOUR. (*Proudly.*) A lion-tamer in the circus.

YVONNE. (*With poorly hidden disgust.*) Really? A lion-tamer?

LATOUR. Oh, Madame—he was handsome. I remember the first time I saw him. I was at the circus—in the front row—with my husband. What a chest he had!

YVONNE. Your husband?

LATOUR. No—the lion-tamer. Oh, he was wonderful! How he whipped those ferocious beasts. I thought to myself: "Imagine how he could whip a woman."

YVONNE. That's terrible! A man who would do that to me— (*She rises and goes toward* R.)

LATOUR. (*Air of connoisseur.*) Don't condemn it until you've tried it. (*Resuming her narrative.*) Well—two weeks later, my lion-tamer received me in an apartment as elegant and as perfumed as this one.

YVONNE. Your lion-tamer was well-off.

LATOUR. (*With an ironic grimace.*) I paid the rent! Oh, Madame, never fall for a lion-tamer from the circus.

YVONNE. I have no intention. (*She sits on the piano bench and leafs through the music which is on the stand.*)

LATOUR. I approve of your choice—a gentleman like Monsieur Roussel.

YVONNE. My relationship with Monsieur Roussel is not what you take it to be.

LATOUR. I beg your pardon. (*She goes a little to* L. *Silence as* YVONNE *figures out a piece on the piano.* LATOUR *listens a moment.*) Good! Very good! Paderewski used that piano.

YVONNE. (*Stopping, looks at her.*) Paderewski? Do you know Paderewski?

LATOUR. (*Swelling with vanity.*) Oh, we often made music together.

YVONNE. (*Astonished.*) No! When?

LATOUR. Before the downfall.

YVONNE. Oh.

LATOUR. (*Bitterly.*) I must say—since I became a concierge, Paderewski hasn't set foot in my house. (YVONNE, *in a manner of consoling her, bends slightly towards* LATOUR, *then turning the piano stool, starts playing the piece. It sounds rather pitiful to* LATOUR.) No—wait. If you will permit me—it's written for four hands.

YVONNE. (*Making room by moving piano stool towards treble.*) Gladly, Countess.

LATOUR. Thank you, Madame, thank you. (*She takes chair from table, places it by piano bass, and sits.*) There! Two measures for a try.

YVONNE. Two measures.

BOTH. One, two, three— (*They attack the piece with four hands.* LATOUR *tries to play very elegantly. After a few measures,* ROUSSEL *enters with a bottle of champagne.*)

ROUSSEL. (*Just coming in the door.*) I found it, Countess. (*He stops, amazed by the scene.*) A piano recital—

at a time like this? (*Then to the two women.*) What's going on here?

YVONNE. (*Without interrupting the music.*) We're playing with four hands. (LATOUR *continues playing.*)

ROUSSEL. My compliments—four hands. How exciting! (*Takes a step.*) Countess! (*She continues playing. He taps bottle on the table for attention.*) Countess! Countess!

LATOUR. (*Half-turning, still playing.*) La, la, la, la, la. Huh? (ROUSSEL *puts the champagne on the table.*)

ROUSSEL. (*Mimicking her.*) Huh! I found the champagne, but where is the ice-bucket?

LATOUR. (*Over her shoulder.*) It should be in the cupboard—or else with the tablecloths and napkins.

ROUSSEL. (*Sarcastic.*) Thanks. Don't disturb yourself.

LATOUR. (*Rises quickly.*) Pardon me. I'll get it.

ROUSSEL. It would pain me to interrupt you. I'll look for it myself. (*He goes out.*)

LATOUR. Thank you, thank you. (*To* YVONNE.) Where were we? Shall we go on?

YVONNE. No—it's too difficult. (*She turns on piano stool, speaks distractedly to* LATOUR.) Your unhappy experience with the lion tamer—was that a long time ago?

LATOUR. (*Above the table, replacing the chair.*) Oh, yes—at least a dozen years. I remember the very day—it was at the feast of the Immaculate Conception.

YVONNE. It's too bad your husband caught you—and on such a day.

LATOUR. Don't talk about it. And to think he used the oldest trick in the world.

YVONNE. Really? What was it?

LATOUR. (*Going to* YVONNE.) The fake departure, Madame—the husband who says he is going hunting.

YVONNE. Hunting?

LATOUR. Yes. Isn't that the oldest trick of all?

YVONNE. (*A sardonic laugh.*) My husband also says he goes hunting. They're all the same.

LATOUR. I don't have to tell you it's not animals they hunt for.

YVONNE. Of course not. It's just a pretext to visit their mistresses.

LATOUR. Oh, no. When a husband wants to visit his mistress, he says he is going to his club—that's standard. But, when he goes hunting—

YVONNE. That doesn't prove that he has a mistress?

LATOUR. No! That proves he is suspicious of his wife, and wants to trap her.

YVONNE. (*Startled.*) Good heavens! (*She rises and paces.*)

LATOUR. What's the matter?

YVONNE. (*Going down* R.) I hadn't ever thought of it like that. But, Countess, what if the husband has used the excuse of going hunting several times before?

LATOUR. That simply means that he has discovered nothing, but he's still on the trail.

YVONNE. That's frightful! And I was thinking— (*She passes* LATOUR *brusquely, goes to door,* L.) Roussel! Roussel? (ROUSSEL *enters with ice-bucket, in jovial spirits.*)

ROUSSEL. What's wrong, my dear?

YVONNE. Quickly—my coat and hat.

ROUSSEL. What?

YVONNE. I can't stay another moment in this apartment.

ROUSSEL. (*Going to her.*) What are you talking about?

YVONNE. I'm talking about your abusing my confidence —making me believe things that are not so.

ROUSSEL. What?

YVONNE. But, thank God, I can still say I'm faithful to my husband.

ROUSSEL. No doubt—no doubt.

YVONNE. And he is faithful to me—the poor dear.

ROUSSEL. Faithful? When he goes to see his mistress under the pretense of hunting?

YVONNE. (*Putting on her hat.*) You know very well

that when a man visits his mistress, he tells his wife he is going to the club. Everyone knows that.

ROUSSEL. So what? The club—or hunting—what's the difference?

YVONNE. The difference is that hunting means the husband is suspicious of his wife and is trying to trap her.

ROUSSEL. What did you do—read the rule-book?

YVONNE. (*Goes to mirror,* L., *to look at hat.*) Ask the Countess—she'll tell you what she told me.

ROUSSEL. Huh? (*He turns, faces* LATOUR *with a murderous look. She backs to door,* R.) You—told—her—that?

LATOUR. (*Babbling.*) I said—I said—oh, I say that all the time.

ROUSSEL. (*Furious.*) Who asked your opinion? Who asked you to meddle in our affairs?

LATOUR. Oh, Monsieur—if I had foreseen—

ROUSSEL. Take care, Countess. (*Raises his hand as if to strike her.* LATOUR *assumes a rigid position as if to receive the blow.*)

YVONNE. (*Still by the mirror.*) Leave the Countess alone! She's not involved in this. I'm leaving because I want to leave, that's all. (*She puts on her coat.*)

ROUSSEL. Not on your life! (*To* LATOUR.) But you can go—and the quicker the better. (LATOUR *hustles out as* ROUSSEL *slams door on her.*) That old gossip! Yvonne, you can't be serious.

YVONNE. You'll see if I'm serious or not.

ROUSSEL. (*With a woe-begone expression.*) But what's come over you? When I left the room to find an ice-bucket, you were quite calm.

YVONNE. (*Arms crossed, tapping her foot.*) Yes.

ROUSSEL. You were perfectly content.

YVONNE. Yes. (*Remembering her dignity.*) I was not!

ROUSSEL. You appeared to be. But when I came back in the room, you had changed completely. What is the explanation?

YVONNE. I don't owe you explanations. I'm going to leave. I'm free, I suppose? (*She goes in direction of door.*)

ROUSSEL. No, you're not free! I have your word—and your word should be sacred. (*He blocks her way, making her go front of sofa.*)

YVONNE. I take back my sacred word! (*She makes a tour of sofa by the* L. *but* ROUSSEL *anticipates, going above sofa at* R., *making her retreat.*)

ROUSSEL. You have given me a mission to fulfill—to avenge you on your husband. I intend to carry out that mission.

YVONNE. (*She runs to* R., *between table and piano, trying to reach door, but* ROUSSEL *blocks her at door.*) You'll see how you avenge me.

ROUSSEL. But, Yvonne—this is cruel. You know that I love you.

YVONNE. (*With a sneer.*) Ha!

ROUSSEL. Yes, I love you. (*Declaims in a supreme effort.*) My heart burns with passion just to hear your name. The tender—

YVONNE. You started that fire before. Throw ashes on it. (*She goes* L.)

ROUSSEL. (*Following.*) You're cruel. You told me you couldn't resist me when I recited poetry.

YVONNE. I can now—and I'll prove it to you— (*She makes a dash for the door but he grabs her wrist, spinning her around and causing her to fall on the sofa.*)

ROUSSEL. (*With energy.*) Yvonne—you are going to stay here!

YVONNE. (*Sitting up, furious.*) Violence!

ROUSSEL. Yes—violence—if it's necessary.

YVONNE. Oh! (*Exasperated, she pushes her hat down on her head.*)

ROUSSEL. You forget that when you came under my roof, your reputation was placed in my care, and I intend to defend it—even against you.

YVONNE. Against me?

ROUSSEL. Yes—you. For your servants—and for all

the world—you are in the country visiting your aunt—
and you're going to stay there. Do you want everyone to
know that your aunt was a hoax? Can't you hear the
gossips?

YVONNE. One time—two times—you won't let me
leave?

ROUSSEL. No! No! No!

YVONNE. (*Taking off her coat.*) Very well—I'll spend
the night on this sofa. (*She puts her coat on back of sofa,
sits, furious.*)

ROUSSEL. As you please. I'll spend the night on this
chair. (*Also angry, he sits at* L. *of table, back half-turned.*
YVONNE *calms her nerves by pounding cushions. He
mumbles, and taps his hand on the table, suddenly real-
inzing he has his hand in the butter. He cleans it off with
a napkin.*) I'll remember this night.

YVONNE. (*Her back to* ROUSSEL.) So shall I.

ROUSSEL. A night of love—on a chair!

YVONNE. (*Over her shoulder.*) Don't make yourself
uncomfortable on my account. Sleep in your bed.

ROUSSEL. And you?

YVONNE. I'll sleep in the other room—on a chair—or
on the floor if necessary.

ROUSSEL. (*Rising.*) I won't allow it. You take the bed.

YVONNE. Sleep in your bed? I wouldn't think of it.

ROUSSEL. But without me, I mean.

YVONNE. (*Rises, goes to fireplace.*) With you, or without you, the result would be the same.

ROUSSEL. (*Off-hand.*) I'd hate to think that! (*He sits*
L. *of table.*)

YVONNE. I shall install myself in the other room, and
I shall sleep—or I shall not sleep. Either way, it will be
my punishment.

ROUSSEL. Good God! And all because of that con—that
concierge. (*Shakes his fist at the door.*)

YVONNE. All I ask is that you give me a blanket.

ROUSSEL. All right! (*He goes to bed, pulls blanket off,*

then changing his mind throws it back in anger.) You'll regret this.

YVONNE. What?

ROUSSEL. It's as cold as the North Pole in there.

YVONNE. Never mind—I'll light a fire. (*She takes her coat and goes toward door,* L.)

ROUSSEL. (*Furious.*) Oh—that Countess!

YVONNE. I'll never be caught at this again! (*She goes in door,* L., *slamming it.*)

ROUSSEL. (*He drags the blanket from the bed, goes downstage with it trailing.*) She thinks she's the only woman in the world. She's not that pretty! (*There is a knock at the door.*) Who is it? (*As he turns he gets tangled up in the blanket, almost falling, then throws it on back of sofa before going to open the door.*)

LATOUR. (*Entering timidly.*) It's the Countess, Monsieur.

ROUSSEL. You again? Haven't I seen enough of you? (*He turns her around as if to shove her out.*)

LATOUR. (*Returning to the charge.*) But, Monsieur, it's the tenant across the hall who sent me to see you.

ROUSSEL. I don't even know him. (*Again he turns her around.*)

LATOUR. I'm aware of that. But his niece had an attack of some sort—her nerves, I think—and since he knew you were a doctor, he—

ROUSSEL. Well, you tell him I'm not a doctor at night. And please leave. You've complicated things enough as it is. (*He pushes her to the door.*)

LATOUR. Thank you, Monsieur. I'll tell him. (*She goes out.*)

ROUSSEL. (*Closing door with a slam, locks it.*) The devil take his niece and her miserable nerves. (YVONNE *enters and appears to be looking for something.*) What are you looking for?

YVONNE. (*Dryly, going to fireplace.*) Matches. I want to light a fire.

ROUSSEL. There—on the fireplace.

YVONNE. I see them—I'm not blind. (*She takes the matches and exits.*)

ROUSSEL. (*Looks after her, stung, then down R. with bitter half-laugh.*) What a sweet character! No wonder her husband goes hunting. (*A knock at door, R.*) Again! Is that you, Countess?

CHANDEL. (*Outside.*) It's not the Countess—it's me—your neighbor.

ROUSELL. More trouble! (*Goes to door, unlocks it, opens it.*) What do you want? (*He recognizes CHANDEL, horrified, leans on door.*)

CHANDEL. (*Without seeing ROUSSEL.*) Monsieur—

ROUSSEL. You can't come in! (*He pushes door quickly, catching CHANDEL's arm in the door.*)

CHANDEL. (*Trying to free his arm.*) Ouch!

ROUSSEL. (*Leaning against the door.*) Oh, my God!

CHANDEL. You're hurting my arm.

ROUSSEL. (*Still leaning on door.*) I told you that you can't come in. (*CHANDEL pushes door with such force that ROUSSEL is thrown into C. of room and bumps into sofa.*) Oh!

CHANDEL. Roussel!

ROUSSEL. (*Affecting surprise.*) Chandel! You! It's good to see you. (*He giggles like an idiot.*)

CHANDEL. (*Rubbing his arm.*) Do you live here?

ROUSSEL. (*Trying to be casual.*) You see that I do. Didn't I tell you?

CHANDEL. No.

ROUSSEL. That's because I took the place only this afternoon.

CHANDEL. Then you must be the doctor?

ROUSSEL. What doctor?

CHANDEL. The doctor who lives here.

ROUSSEL. (*Affecting a laugh.*) Oh, yes—I'm the doctor—I'm the doctor.

CHANDEL. Is anything wrong with you?

ROUSSEL. Me? Nothing—nothing. (*Noise of fireplace damper in room at L. makes ROUSSEL shudder.*)

CHANDEL. (*Indicating other room.*) Who's in there?

ROUSSEL. The chimney-sweep.

CHANDEL. At this hour?

ROUSSEL. He's a night chimney-sweep—works only at night—you know, like an owl. (*Goes to door, L., locks it.*)

CHANDEL. Why did you lock the door?

ROUSSEL. Because of the soot—to keep the soot out.

CHANDEL. Tell the truth, my friend—you've come across something special, haven't you?

ROUSSEL. Me?

CHANDEL. There's nothing to be ashamed of. Don't you think I noticed that table set for two? Ah, ha!

ROUSSEL. It was there when I rented the apartment. Meals are furnished. American plan.

CHANDEL. Now, now—no more alibis. I've already been told that you have a rendezvous with someone's wife.

ROUSSEL. You know?

CHANDEL. Yes.

ROUSSEL. Who told you?

CHANDEL. Madame Latour, the concierge.

ROUSSEL. Oh, yes—Countess Bigmouth. Yes, I'll confess, I've had a stroke of good luck—a woman is in that room.

CHANDEL. Of course. (*Taking his arm.*) Who is the happy victim?

ROUSSEL. Please—be discreet.

CHANDEL. (*Childishly.*) But you can tell *me*.

ROUSSEL. No—especially not you.

CHANDEL. Are you afraid I might talk?

ROUSSEL. No—I'm sure you wouldn't talk this time.

CHANDEL. Well—confess—who is it?

ROUSSEL. It's—uh—uh—it's Madame Castillo.

CHANDEL. (*Laughing, gives* ROUSSEL *a push.*) You're joking!

ROUSSEL. Word of honor!

CHANDEL. Now, now, Roussel— (*Very confidentially.*) I'm with *her*.

ROUSSEL. What? You're—? (*His mouth open wide as*

things begin to sink in. He goes mechanically to sofa, spreads the blanket on sofa back, pats it down, laughing in idiotic fashion.)

CHANDEL. So you have no confidence in me. Anyhow, I'm happy that the doctor turned out to be you. I'll take you to Madame Castillo. She's taken ill. (*Takes* ROUSSEL'S *arm, tries to lead him to door.*)

ROUSSEL. Where is she?

CHANDEL. Across the hall. I'll meet you there—but first I want to borrow some smelling salts from the concierge. (*He is about to leave when there is a loud pounding on door at* L., *followed by an intense reaction from* ROUSSEL.) Your chimney-sweep wants out. (*He laughs heartily at this.*)

ROUSSEL. I know—but not now. (*Nervously, he goes to the door. Suddenly a voice says "ROUSSEL," but he immediately pounces on the door and beats on it. Then he starts singing "Evening Star" from Tannhäuser loud enough to burst a blood vessel, beating on the door in tempo.*)

"Oh, thou sublime, sweet evening star,
  Joyful I greet thee from afar."

CHANDEL. (*Puts his arm on* ROUSSEL'S *shoulder.*) Once more—together.

BOTH. (*Facing audience.*)

Oh, thou sublime, sweet evening star,
Joyful I greet thee from afar.

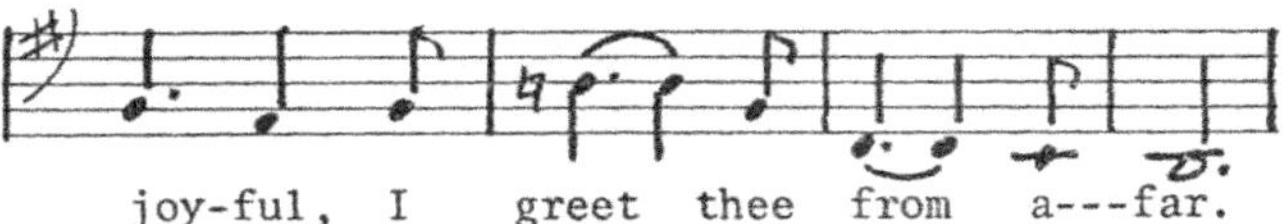

CHANDEL. (*Laughing merrily.*) We sound great together. But I have no more time to waste. I'm going down to the concierge. You take care of Madame Castillo—do you hear? (ROUSSEL, *still singing, signifies "yes" with head.* CHANDEL *exits.* ROUSSEL *slams door behind him, then leans his back against the door and drops to the floor.*)

ROUSSEL. I wish I were in Siberia.

YVONNE. (*In other room.*) Open the door! (*She pounds on door.*)

ROUSSEL. Coming! Coming! (*He leaps up, goes to door, unlocks it.*)

YVONNE. (*Furious.*) What kind of joke was that— locking me in, and yelling at me like a maniac?

ROUSSEL. I was only trying to save your life.

YVONNE. What did you say?

ROUSSEL. I haven't time to explain now. I must leave for a moment. In the name of heaven, don't show yourself. If anyone knocks—don't speak—and don't open the door—except to me. (*He goes out.*)

YVONNE. (*Talking at door as if* ROUSSEL *could hear.*) Roussel! Where are you going? Come back here! (*Turns angrily.*) I know what I'm going to do. I'm going into the next room, I'm going to get my coat, and I'll go down and ask the concierge what's going on here. (*She goes out* L., *muttering.*) What a night! What a night! (*She has just closed the door when* CHANDEL *rushes in,* R., *with a bottle of smelling salts in his hand.*)

CHANDEL. I've got the smelling salts. Roussel! (*Goes to door,* L.) Are you in there, Roussel? (*He hears a noise in the room.*) Someone is in there. (*Knocks at door.*) Roussel! Roussel! (*He strides nervously to* R.)

(CHANDEL *is examining the food on the table as* YVONNE *enters with coat on. She immediately recognizes her husband.*)

YVONNE. (*In a hoarse whisper.*) Oh, my God—my husband! (*Frightened, she casts a rapid glance around the room, wondering where she can hide. Suddenly she sees within easy reach, the blanket which* ROUSSEL *put on the back of the sofa. Hastily she seizes the blanket and drapes it over her entire body just as* CHANDEL *turns around. He looks at her, amazed.*)

CHANDEL. What's that? A ghost? (YVONNE *takes a step to* L.) It walks! (*She is about to bump into the fireplace.*) Careful! You'll be burned like Joan of Arc. (*She recoils. Tries to grope her way to door,* L.) Madame, don't be afraid. I respect your incognito. I simply wanted to know if the doctor is still here. Is he? (*She shakes her head several times negatively.*) He left? (*She shakes her head in accord.*) Will you pardon the intrusion, please? (*Again shaking head.*) Thank you, Madame, I'll be leaving now. (YVONNE *takes a bow.*) Sorry to have bothered you. (*She motions a kick under blanket and almost falls in a heap, tangled in the blanket, but she gets control and sits on sofa, still covered as* ROUSSEL *comes in from* R.) Oh, here you are.

ROUSSEL. Are you still here? (*Sees* YVONNE *on sofa. He leaps, in order to stand between her and* CHANDEL, *crying out in alarm.*) Oh!

CHANDEL. What's the matter? Oh, I see. (*Points to* YVONNE, *begins to laugh.* ROUSSEL *tries to laugh also.*) But tell me—have you been there yet?

ROUSSEL. No—no—what? Been where?

CHANDEL. To see the patient.

ROUSSEL. Oh, her? Nothing wrong. I gave her a pill— and don't allow her to drink so much wine. She's waiting for you—go—go. (*Pushes him toward the door.*)

CHANDEL. (*Resisting a little.*) I understand—you're anxious to—oh, ho, she must be charming—this conquest of yours. A real cover-girl.

ROUSSEL. Will you please leave?

CHANDEL. I'll leave. (*He goes toward* YVONNE.) Au revoir, Madame. (YVONNE *rises, makes a gesture.* CHANDEL *goes to door, then turns.*) Good luck to you, Casanova.

ROUSSEL. (*Rushing to door to push him out.*) Thanks!

(*As he starts to lock the door,* CHANDEL *sticks his head in.*)

CHANDEL. Think about me—won't you? (*He laughs and* ROUSSEL *slams door in his face, locks door and again leans wearily against it.*)

ROUSSEL. Ouf!

YVONNE. (*Cautiously removing blanket and sinking on sofa.*) Is he gone?

ROUSSEL. Yes.

YVONNE. I was almost frightened to death. What are we going to do? (*She rolls the blanket, but distractedly.*) We'd better leave now.

ROUSSEL. Leave? Never! Especially, not now.

YVONNE. Do you think I want to be here while my husband is—?

ROUSSEL. That's the point. If we left now, we might meet him in the hall, or on the stairs. Here at least, we're safe. (*Goes to door.*) The door is locked. I'll put the key on the night-stand—and no one can come in. (*He puts key on night-stand.*)

YVONNE. (*Rising, with rolled blanket, goes little to* R.) Anything will be better than all this excitement. (*She lets her head fall on the blanket as if it were a pillow. She is sleeping, standing up.*)

ROUSSEL. Courage, my love. The danger has passed now. What we must try to do is to sleep until morning. Then you can go calmly to your home as if you were really returning from a visit in the country. (*He goes toward bed.*)

YVONNE. Do you think I can sleep at a time like this? (*She goes to door,* L.)

ROUSSEL. Try! I'm going to try. Good night. (*He takes off jacket, puts it on* seat *of chair by bed.*)

YVONNE. Good night! I'll never forgive you for this. (*She storms out, taking the blanket.*)

ROUSSEL. (*Before she has even shut the door.*) Oh, pooh!

YVONNE. (*Immediately reappearing.*) What did you say?

ROUSSEL. (*To tune of "Under the Bridges of Paris."*) Poo-poo-poo-poo-poo-poo, poo-poo-poo-poo-poo-poo. I can never remember the words.

YVONNE. Oh! (*She goes back into room,* L.)

ROUSSEL. (*Takes off vest, puts it on chair, unfastens suspenders.*) Well, here we are! Is there anything more ridiculous than a squashed lover? I should stick to removing adenoids. Seduction isn't my line. (*Takes off shoes as he sits on chair.*) That stubborn female is going to be very uncomfortable in there. And all because she thinks of nothing but her husband. What does he have to do with us? He's playing his own little game across the hall. (*Takes off trousers, rises, puts them on* back *of chair.*) So, this is what they call a night of love. Well, Roussel, you imbecile, you deserve it—so enjoy it. Get to bed, and have a sweet dream. (*Turns out lamp, crawls into bed, pulls covers over him.*) The devil take all women! Who needs them? (YVONNE *enters and goes to sofa.*)

YVONNE. Are you already in bed? (*She tries various cushions for softness.*)

ROUSSEL. I found nothing more exciting to do.

YVONNE. (*Nervously plumping cushion.*) Oh, you men! When you're deprived of your pleasures, nothing else matters.

ROUSSEL. (*Sitting up in bed.*) Did you come back just to tell me *that?*

YVONNE. No! I came back to get a cushion which I intend to put under my head.

ROUSSEL. Well? Do you have it?

YVONNE. Yes, I have it. (*Goes toward him.*) Little it matters to you that I will spend the night on a chair. You're well tucked-in.

ROUSSEL. Now, look here, Yvonne.

YVONNE. Sleep, my friend—sleep with a clear conscience. (ROUSSEL *pulls sheet over his head muttering.* YVONNE *moves down by sofa, facing front.*) An honest woman—a faithful wife—almost ruined her reputation because of you. If it hadn't been for that lucky blanket, it would have happened. Before the whole world, I would have been a fallen woman. (ROUSSEL *titters,* YVONNE *swings around to the bed.*) Can you lie there and tell me you're an honorable man? Can you? Well? (*Closer to bed.*) Dare to tell me you're an honorable man! (ROUSSEL, *asleep, responds with a hearty snore.*) Asleep! No conscience whatsoever! (*She is about to throw the cushion at his head, changes her mind, goes out* L. *in anger. Stage is silent a moment, then we hear a key turn in door,* R. PIERRE *enters quietly.*)

PIERRE. Fifi! Fifi! Don't be afraid—it's me—Pierre. She must be asleep. (*Heavy breathing from bed.*) The poor thing must have a cold. (*Goes to door which he left open, locks it, starts to put key in pocket, then looks at it fondly.*) I'm a lucky student to have a key like this. I've learned a lot with it. It opened the door to higher education. And the course I've had here is much more interesting than algebra. But Fifi is a very strict teacher. Sometimes she makes me repeat the lesson over and over —but I never complain. (*Turns toward bed.*) Fifi! Still sleeping—and after I sent her a message that I was coming for an extra lesson. (ROUSSEL *snores.*) She has a terrible cold. I'll wake her up with a kiss. What nicer way could I use to awaken my dear teacher? (*Climbs into bed, lies next to* ROUSSEL, *kisses him.*)

ROUSSEL. (*Half-asleep.*) Who is it?

PIERRE. (*Sitting up.*) A man!

ROUSSEL. (*Still groggy.*) Yvonne, is that you? (*He puts his arms around* PIERRE'S *neck.*)

PIERRE. (*Terrified.*) Let go of me! (*They struggle in the bed, their cries mix and pillows and bolster fly. There is an enormous racket after which* PIERRE *slides into space between bed and wall.*)

ROUSSEL. (*Leaping out of bed, half-crazy, groping in the dark.*) Who's here? Where are you? I saw you! It was a man! (*Looks toward door,* L.) Oh! Yvonne! He must have gone in there. (*Dashes into room,* L.)

YVONNE. (*In other room, screams.*) What do you want?

PIERRE. (*Crawls out from under the bed.*) That must be the monkey! (*He runs to the closet, down* L., *and goes in.* ROUSSEL, *like a madman, rushes in, followed by an equally agitated* YVONNE.)

ROUSSEL. I tell you there was a man in here.

YVONNE. But where? Where?

ROUSSEL. I don't know! Let's look for him.

(*They look around,* ROUSSEL *extreme* R., YVONNE *near bed.* ROUSSEL *turns on the lamp.*)

YVONNE. You frightened me out of my wits. Where did you see a man?

ROUSSEL. There—in my bed. He kissed me. (*On all fours, he looks under the bed, as* YVONNE *looks under the sofa.*)

YVONNE. You're raving mad. You had a nightmare.

ROUSSEL. I know when I've had a nightmare—and I know when I've been kissed.

YVONNE. (*Inspecting the door,* R.) Look—the door is locked. He couldn't have come in through the keyhole.

ROUSSEL. (*Goes to join* YVONNE *at door.*) Is the door locked?

YVONNE. (*Holding the door-knob to show him.*) See for yourself.

ROUSSEL. (*Tries it.*) It's impossible.

YVONNE. Do you think you've gone crazy?

ROUSSEL. I tell you, I'm not crazy—and I'm not delirious. I felt it here. (*Points to his cheek.*) And I can still feel it.

YVONNE. It was only a nightmare.

ROUSSEL. A nightmare?

YVONNE. Yes.

ROUSSEL. (*Tries to laugh.*) A nightmare.

YVONNE. (*Sitting in chair at table.*) It's not funny, my

friend—not funny at all. You have no right to do this to me.

RoussEL. I'm sorry—forgive me. (*He sinks on the sofa.*) I really thought I saw him.

YvonnE. What a nightI What a night!

RoussEL. Yes—what a night! I could have done without it.

(*There is a moment of silence as they sit glaring at each other. Then, a loud knock at door, R. The knocks are very regular and each knock makes them shiver.*)

YvonnE. Someone is knocking.

RoussEL. (*Rising quickly, stands R. of sofa.*) I heard.

VoicE. (*Outside.*) Open—in the name of the law!

RoussEL. Police! (RoussEL *leaps two feet, straight up, then both run like frightened rabbits as the knocking continues.*) Hide yourself!

YvonnE. Where? Where? (*She opens door, L.*) There's no way out of this room.

VoicE. (*Outside.*) Open, or I'll be forced to break down the door.

YvonnE. In the bed! (*She jumps in the bed.*)

RoussEL. Not there—that's the first place they'll look. (*She gets out of bed, runs to window.*)

YvonnE. The window?

RoussEL. Too far to the ground!

YvonnE. (*Clutching* RoussEL.) Please—what can I do?

RoussEL. I don't know—but for heaven's sake—move!

VoicE. (*Outside.*) We know you're in there—no use to try to run.

RoussEL. Yes, yes—coming! (*To* YvonnE *who has moved near fireplace.*) All we can do is to keep cool, calm, and dignified. (*He puts on his jacket, forgetting his trousers.*) My hat! My hat! (*Points to hat which* YvonnE *tosses to him.*) Just say what I say.

VoicE. (*Outside.*) Are you going to open the door of your own free will?

ROUSSEL. Come in! Come in! (*Opens door,* DUVAL, *in plain clothes, enters, then turns his head towards door.*)

DUVAL. You men wait for me there.

ROUSSEL. (*A sharp cry as if he had forgotten something.*) Oh! (*Grabs gloves from night-stand and nonchalantly puts them on.*) Please tell me what warrant allows you to force my door at this hour?

DUVAL. (*Politely, taking off hat.*) I'm going to tell you. But first, I ask your pardon for this intrusion. As a policeman, I do my duty—as a gentleman, I present my apology.

ROUSSEL. Well, Inspector—I'm waiting. (YVONNE *silently slips a cushion to* ROUSSEL *which he holds in front of him to cover himself.*)

DUVAL. Monsieur, I come at the request of your husband— (*Stops, takes a step downstage, speaks to* YVONNE.) Pardon me. Madame, I come at the request of your husband to verify the presence of this man in your dwelling place at this hour.

ROUSSEL. But, Monsieur—I don't understand. I am married—and this is my wife.

DUVAL. (*Sarcastic.*) I know—I know—they all say that. As a man, I approve of your chivalry, but as a police officer, I say—well, never mind. What is your name?

ROUSSEL. Doctor Roussel.

DUVAL. (*Writing.*) And yours, Madame?

YVONNE. I'm Madame Doctor Roussel.

ROUSSEL. She's my wife, I told you.

DUVAL. Don't be stubborn—we know very well this is not Madame Roussel.

YVONNE. Oh, my God!

DUVAL. This is Madame Castillo.

YVONNE and ROUSSEL. Madame Castillo?

DUVAL. That is correct—Madame Castillo. And it is because you are Madame Castillo that I am here.

ROUSSEL. Madame Castillo! Did you hear that? He said "Madame Castillo." (*Tries to embrace* DUVAL *who pushes him away*.) Oh, my dear man—my lovely man—Madame Castillo lives across the hall.

DUVAL. Across the hall?

ROUSSEL. Of course, Monsieur, across the hall.

DUVAL. (*Back to audience.*) Permit me—the concierge said "second floor—door on the right." This is my right, I believe. (*He extends his right hand.*)

ROUSSEL. (*Turning the Inspector to face audience.*) The stairway has a double turn. You see—your right is there. (*He lifts Inspector's arm and points it towards door.*)

DUVAL. Oh, Monsieur, I got turned around—my left became my right.

ROUSSEL. You don't wake up people at this hour to tell them that.

DUVAL. Monsieur, I am desolate. Madame— (*He starts for door.*) Continue—as you were. (*He leaves.* ROUSSEL *slams the door shut.*)

ROUSSEL. "Continue—as you were." Continue what? Our mad affair?

DUVAL. (*Outside.*) It's across the hall.

YVONNE. (*Sitting on sofa.*) Oh, this is too much.

ROUSSEL. Yvonne!

YVONNE. What?

ROUSSEL. This is really too much.

YVONNE. I just said that.

ROUSSEL. I didn't hear you. (*Sits* R. *of table.*)

YVONNE. Police—imagine! You think of everything for your little parties.

ROUSSEL. Its not my fault. They were looking for Madame Castillo. Didn't I send them to Madame Castillo?

YVONNE. (*Furious.*) Yes!

ROUSSEL. (*Strikes his forehead, rising at same time.*) Oh, good God!

YVONNE. What is it?

ROUSSEL. If he goes in there, he will—he will—he will— (*He can't say it. Tries to pantomime the gravity of* CHANDEL'S *situation, making ridiculous jerks of hands and legs, and almost dancing from the door to the sofa and back again.*)

YVONNE. Are you happy with what happened?

ROUSSEL. No, I'm not happy. Do I look happy?

YVONNE. Yes—you're dancing. (*Starts to door,* L.) Oh, that man! (*She disappears.*)

ROUSSEL. Now—you listen to me, Yvonne— (*He follows her into room,* L., *as* CHANDEL *appears on balcony and crawls in window. He has his hat and coat on, very sloppily, but no trousers. He has his gun and cartridge belt. He looks around.*)

CHANDEL. My God! I forgot my trousers! How can I get out of here like this? (*He sees* ROUSSEL'S *trousers on chair, slips them on quickly as* PIERRE *comes out of closet.*)

PIERRE. It seems quiet in here now. (*Sees* CHANDEL.) My uncle! (*Dashes back into closet.*)

CHANDEL. Pierre! (*He runs to door, turns key which* ROUSSEL *left in keyhole, and scurries out. At this moment two policemen in plain clothes appear on balcony and enter room. Alarmed by the noise the policemen made when entering,* ROUSSEL *enters from room,* L.)

ROUSSEL. What's all that noise?

FIRST POLICEMAN. (*Sees* ROUSSEL *and starts in pursuit.*) There he is—the man in his shorts. That's the one.

ROUSSEL. Who are you people?

FIRST POLICEMAN. (*Rushing him.*) Come on—you!

ROUSSEL. (*Saving himself, pursued by the two men.*) Leave me alone! What do you want with me? (*A general chase. Finally, after a race in every direction,* ROUSSEL, *having made a tour of the table from the* R. *to escape the first man, goes rear and is nabbed by the second man. The first man quickly joins.*)

THE TWO POLICEMEN. We have him!

ROUSSEL. (*Shouting.*) Let me go!

SECOND POLICEMAN. (*Restraining him with help of the*

other man.) This will teach you to run out on balconies in your underwear.

ROUSSEL. (*Struggling while being literally carried.*) Will you let go of me! You're crazy! Help! Help!

FIRST POLICEMAN. You can explain everything to the Inspector. (*They carry him out the door, in spite of his resistance.*)

YVONNE. (*Frightened, rushes in from room, L.*) What's happening?

PIERRE. (*Slipping out of closet, recognizes YVONNE.*) My aunt!

YVONNE. Pierre! (*In terror, she runs out the door, R. PIERRE stands there looking bewildered.*)

CURTAIN

END OF ACT TWO

ACT THREE

Same scene as Act One. Next morning. The stage is empty. A doorbell is heard. After a moment, the rear door opens to reveal ROUSSEL *and* BABETTE.

ROUSSEL. Is Madame here?

BABETTE. (*At rear.*) Yes. She arrived home from the country on an early train.

ROUSSEL. And Monsieur?

BABETTE. He hasn't returned from his hunting trip. But here is Madame Chandel. (*Seeing* YVONNE *enter from* R.)

YVONNE. You may leave now, Babette.

BABETTE. Yes, Madame. (*She goes out, rear.*)

YVONNE. So! Here you are. (*They both come down.*)

ROUSSEL. Yvonne, I didn't dare come any earlier—but what anxiety I've had. I've been wondering what became of you after last night's horrible escapade.

YVONNE. I don't yet know what became of me! When I found that you had disappeared, I lost my head. I didn't know what I was doing. The room was a shambles—the window was wide open—the door was open. And then— to make the whole thing like a bad dream—Pierre came bouncing out of the closet.

ROUSSEL. Pierre? What was Pierre doing there?

YVONNE. How do I know what Pierre was doing there? I don't even know what *I* was doing there. I thought I was delirious—or insane. I ran out the door—down the stairs—into the street—without my hat or coat—and without looking back.

ROUSSEL. (*With commiseration.*) Oh, la, la.

YVONNE. I don't know how long I walked in a daze— but I was suddenly brought back to reality when some young night owl comes up to me and says: "Madame, I have twenty francs." (*A slight pause.*) Tell me, Roussel —why did he say he had twenty francs?

Roussel. Perhaps he wanted some change.

Yvonne. Well, no matter. But I knew I couldn't wander around the streets alone.

Roussel. But did you come home at that hour of the night?

Yvonne. I wasn't that insane.

Roussel. What did you do?

Yvonne. I hailed a carriage.

Roussel. But where did you go?

Yvonne. Where can one go at that hour? I told him to drive around the Place de la Concorde until I told him to stop. He thought I was a lunatic—and so did I. But I paid him by the hour and he drove and drove—until morning. I know every statue in the Place de la Concorde by heart—Bordeaux, Marseille, Lyon, Strasbourg, Lille, Rouen, Brest, Nantes, Bordeaux— (*She sits near fireplace.*)

Roussel. You passed Bordeaux already. You're home now. Oh, my poor, sweet Yvonne. At least, I hope you got my message explaining everything.

Yvonne. Yes—I understand it all now. And to think that you were trying to convince me that a husband who pretends to go hunting is not going to see his mistress.

Roussel. Me? How can you say that?

Yvonne. He was with Madame Castillo. Imagine his nerve—using her husband as an alibi.

Roussel. It's not only that. Your husband was doing the hunting, but I was the one the game warden arrested.

Yvonne. (*Rising.*) That was your fault. The Inspector had seen you only a few minutes before. You should have been able to explain the situation to him.

Roussel. Did you ever try to explain something to a Police Inspector? He probably thought I had a woman in both apartments. He said to me: (*Imitating* Duval's *voice.*) "I'm here to state facts, not listen to explanations. A man was in the room with Madame Castillo. He escaped on the balcony—without his trousers. My men trailed him into another apartment. There they caught a man—also without his trousers. It appeared to be the same man. You can explain to the judge." (*He imitates the Inspector's derisive laugh.*)

YVONNE. You should have insisted.

ROUSSEL. I couldn't—he was in a hurry—he was going to the mayor's ball. But I'll settle the matter. I'll call the Inspector, and have him confront your husband. Once they are face to face, they can put things straight.

YVONNE. Yes—that's what you must do.

ROUSSEL. Why should I sacrifice myself for your husband? If you and I had been caught together, do you believe he would have been charitable? I should say not.

YVONNE. That's true. Well, I know there's only one thing for me to do, and that is to get a divorce.

ROUSSEL. Really?

YVONNE. Of course. Don't you think I have sufficient grounds? As long as he knows nothing about my escapade of last night.

ROUSSEL. He doesn't know a thing. You're in the clear.

YVONNE. And to keep it that way, I wish you would return the letter I wrote to you yesterday.

ROUSSEL. Do you really want it? I'd like to keep it. It's the only thing I have of yours.

YVONNE. No—you must return it—I insist.

ROUSSEL. (*Going through his pockets.*) Let's see—where did I put it? (*A look of fright.*) Good God!

YVONNE. What is it?

ROUSSEL. It's in the pocket of my trousers.

YVONNE. Well?

ROUSSEL. Your husband is wearing my trousers.

YVONNE. Oh! We're in fine shape! Do you know that if you had done everything on purpose, it couldn't have gone worse? (*She goes* R.)

ROUSSEL. How was I to know that your husband would steal my trousers?

YVONNE. (*At fireplace.*) You never know anything!

What if my husband has found that letter? And has read it?

Roussel. He couldn't do a sneaky thing like that. They were not *his* trousers.

Yvonne. You don't know what he might do.

Roussel. You're a woman—you'll come up with some explanation.

Yvonne. (*Closing in on him.*) Oh, yes? What?

Roussel. Well—for example—you might say that you —you might say that he— (*Extends left hand, then right.*)

Yvonne. (*Shakes hands with him.*) Thanks!

Roussel. Well—something like that.

Yvonne. Oh, leave me alone—you're no help to me.

Roussel. In that case, I'm going to talk to the Inspector. I have an appointment with him.

Yvonne. Yes—go—go. (Roussel *leaves,* Yvonne *talks to audience.*) That man is exasperating with his lack of foresight. When a man has a letter from a woman— one that can compromise her—he doesn't stuff it into his trousers pocket. A sensible man would ask himself: "What would happen if the husband was wearing my trousers?" Yes, a *sensible* man would. That should have been clear to him. But, no! He thinks of nothing. What am I going to tell my husband if he has found my letter? (*Imitating* Roussel.) "You'll come up with some explanation" he says. But that just won't do. If I make one false step, I could lose a game that I was winning. (*Sitting at table,* L.) Oh, no, no. It's impossible.

Babette. (*Entering from rear.*) Madame, I've just seen Monsieur stepping out of his carriage.

Yvonne. Monsieur?

Babette. Yes, Madame.

Yvonne. (*With a significant look.*) All right—open the door for him. (Babette *exits.*) I'll be able to tell in a minute if he's read my letter—and if he hasn't—oh, la, la—Monsieur Chandel, I'm going to have some fun with you—I'm going to make you squirm—squirm.

BABETTE. (*Comes back in and remains.*) Here is Monsieur Chandel. (CHANDEL, *dressed as in Act One, but with* ROUSSEL'S *trousers, gun case on shoulder, comes in. He is holding a large basket in his hands, which he holds out to be seen, as high as his head.*)

CHANDEL. Yvonne! Where are you, Yvonne? (*He puts the basket on console at* R.)

YVONNE. So you're back?

CHANDEL. Yes, Yvonne, my darling. (*Goes to her and kisses her.*) I'm very happy to see you.

YVONNE. (*Aside.*) He doesn't know anything.

CHANDEL. (*Walking away, aside.*) She doesn't know anything.

YVONNE. Are you tired from your hunt?

CHANDEL. Not at all—not at all. It was invigorating. We bagged a fine lot. It was a great hunt—imagine— from seven in the evening until—

BABETTE. (*At* R. *of table.*) Weren't you cold, Monsieur?

CHANDEL. Huh? Cold? No, I was very hot.

YVONNE. You were hot?

CHANDEL. Yes—I mean my clothes kept me warm. And besides, I was very active.

YVONNE. Of course.

CHANDEL. Castillo wanted me to stay longer, but I was anxious to get back. It's strange—the moment I'm away from you—

YVONNE. Really?

CHANDEL. Yes. I told him I must return to my adorable wife. (*He kisses her.*) It was a great hunt. Beautiful weather.

YVONNE. (*Casually.*) Is that why you changed your trousers? (*Sits* L. *of table.*)

CHANDEL. (*Looks at trousers, thinking fast.*) Yes. The others got soaked. (*Realizing he is contradicting himself.*) You see, the weather was beautiful later, but for an hour it rained torrents. Castillo lent me a pair of his trousers.

YVONNE. I see.

CHANDEL. They don't fit too well, as you can see. But rather than catch cold— (*To* BABETTE.) Will you bring me a pair of trousers from my closet?

BABETTE. Yes, Monsieur. (*She goes out,* L.)

CHANDEL. (*Passing above table, goes down* R.) Oh, it was a fine hunt—you have no idea.

YVONNE. (*Elbows on table, hands on chin, with an air of raillery.*) Oh, I can imagine.

CHANDEL. Do you know that I performed a remarkable feat? I had a double.

YVONNE. (*Pretending great wonderment.*) A double— oh, la, la!

CHANDEL. Yes. I was aiming at a rabbit, when a pheasant flew out of the brush—and bang! I got both with one shot. It killed Castillo.

YVONNE. (*Horrified.*) You killed Castillo?

CHANDEL. I don't mean literally. But I want you to see what I brought. (*He takes basket and puts it on table.*) Have you a pair of scissors?

YVONNE. I'll get them. I'm curious to see the result of your hunt—Tartuffe. (*Goes out,* R., *on that last word.*)

CHANDEL. (*Downstage, near* C.) Those pheasants cost me forty francs. I'd better burn the bill before my wife gets her hands on it. (*Reaches in trousers pocket, brings out* YVONNE'S *letter, looks at it.*) That's not it—that's my wife's handwriting. (*Quickly puts it in* coat *pocket and brings the bill from other trousers pocket.*) This is it. Into the fire! (*Throws the paper in fireplace, returns to sit at* L., *near desk as* YVONNE *enters with scissors and begins to cut string on basket.*)

YVONNE. Are you positive all of this is from your hunt?

CHANDEL. Of course.

YVONNE. Somehow, you don't seem like a man returning from a hunt.

CHANDEL. Are you going to continue what you started yesterday? Didn't I tell you about my famous shot? Didn't I bring you this basket of game?

YVONNE. Is it rabbits and hares?

CHANDEL. Not this time. It's delectable pheasants. But open it—you'll see—open it.

YVONNE. That's what I'm doing. (*She has removed cover and is looking in basket.*) My compliments! You bagged all this?

CHANDEL. Of course.

YVONNE. (*Lifting a bowl of pâté from the basket.*) This?

CHANDEL. (*Stupified, rises.*) Huh?

YVONNE. (*Lifting another bowl, then another.*) And this? And this? All this is from your hunt?

CHANDEL. (*At a loss for words.*) But—

YVONNE. Not only did you shoot a double, but you shot birds that were already plucked, cooked, and made into a pâté.

CHANDEL. You know how birds get in stormy weather.

YVONNE. Think of a better story.

CHANDEL. I'm going to tell you the truth—I wanted to surprise you. I had the birds dressed and made into pâté after the hunt. Think of the work it will save you. (*He goes to basket, hardly believing what is in there. Takes out another bowl.*) Yes, I think it was a brilliant idea.

YVONNE. You're an expert liar but I don't believe one word.

CHANDEL. Now, listen to me, Yvonne—you must believe me.

YVONNE. But I don't!

CHANDEL. Oh!

YVONNE. And as for Castillo, not only was he not with you—but he has never been hunting in his life.

CHANDEL. Who told you such a thing?

YVONNE. Castillo told me such a thing. (*She goes down L. of table.*)

CHANDEL. When was he here?

YVONNE. Yesterday—just after you left. Does that surprise you?

CHANDEL. Not at all. Didn't you notice his strange

manner? He had a sun-stroke when he was in Africa. It affected his memory. When you asked him if he ever went hunting, he naturally said "no," because he doesn't remember that he goes hunting. Castillo loves to hunt. I wish he were here right now. He'd remember yesterday's hunt—I assure you he would. I wish he were here.

(BABETTE *enters from rear.*)

BABETTE. Monsieur Castillo to see you. (CHANDEL *almost caves in.*)

YVONNE. Well—are you satisfied? (CASTILLO *enters.*)

CASTILLO. Buenos días, Señora—buenos días, mi amigo.

CHANDEL. (*Descends on him, whispering, takes him right of table.*) Not a word!

CASTILLO. What? (BABETTE *exits.*)

CHANDEL. (*Hand on* CASTILLO'S *shoulder.*) My good friend Castillo. (*Whispering.*) We hunted together! (*Aloud.*) How have you been since this morning?

CASTILLO. Very well—since this morning, since yesterday, since the day before—

CHANDEL. (*Laughing.*) Oh, yes!

(YVONNE *forces herself between* CHANDEL *and* CASTILLO.)

YVONNE. My husband especially means since this morning—when he left you at the hunt.

CASTILLO. (*Not understanding.*) ¿Mande?

CHANDEL. (*Making desperate signs behind* YVONNE'S *back.*) You know—the hunt!

CASTILLO. The hunt?

CHANDEL. Don't you remember my double? Bang! A rabbit and a pheasant.

YVONNE. Of course he must remember. Look, Monsieur Castillo—here's the result of the slaughter. (*She takes* CASTILLO'S *hand, leads him to table. He looks in basket.*)

CASTILLO. But those are pâtés.

YVONNE. My husband bagged them all.

CASTILLO. (*Laughing.*) Do you shoot pâtés now?

YVONNE. Nobody but *my* husband can do that!

CHANDEL. Why are you playing the fool? You know very well that—

CASTILLO. What?

YVONNE. That you were hunting with him.

CASTILLO. Me?

CHANDEL. Yes—you!

CASTILLO. But, no, Madame.

YVONNE. No? (*She goes* L. *of table.*)

CHANDEL. You see, Yvonne—what did I tell you? His sun-stroke. He doesn't remember a thing.

CASTILLO. My sun-stroke?

CHANDEL. Of course! How could you remember your sun-stroke when your sun-stroke is what destroyed your memory? (*Sees* YVONNE *with arms crossed, shaking her head and muttering.*) What's wrong with *you* now?

YVONNE. Nothing. I'm admiring your talent as a story-teller.

CHANDEL. Me?

YVONNE. Yes—you're remarkable. But you must have a meager opinion of me to think I would swallow such stories. (*She goes down* L. CASTILLO *wanders around, feeling very much in the way.*)

CHANDEL. Yvonne, I assure you.

YVONNE. Do you think that I don't know everything? That your hunting trips are simply pretexts for seeing your women friends? At least, admit your mistakes—then I can say: "He may be unfaithful, but he *is* a man." (*She strides to* R. *and pulls bell-cord.*)

CHANDEL. Now listen to me, Yvonne.

YVONNE. Leave me alone—you exasperate me. (BABETTE *enters, with* CHANDEL'S *trousers on her arm.*)

BABETTE. Did Madame ring?

YVONNE. Yes. Take that basket out of here.

BABETTE. Yes, Madame. (*To* CHANDEL.) Here are the trousers you asked for. I pressed them. (*She goes to basket, looks in it.*) What's this?

YVONNE. My husband shot all those—all by himself.

(*To* CHANDEL, *speaking loud, as if he were deaf.*) Next time, you should patronize a grocer who isn't hard of hearing!

CHANDEL. Yvonne!

YVONNE. No! (*She goes out* R., *slamming the door.* BABETTE *goes out rear with basket, giggling.*)

CHANDEL. (*To* CASTILLO *who is seated on desk chair.*) Triple idiot! Don't you know when to shut up?

CASTILLO. What? What did I say?

CHANDEL. Don't you understand anything? Couldn't you guess that I used you as an excuse—that I had said I went hunting with you?

CASTILLO. Why did you do that?

CHANDEL. Because—because—it's none of your business why I did it. (*Takes off coat, lays it on table.*)

CASTILLO. Ah? (CHANDEL *on his last words, turns a chair with back to audience, sits and starts changing trousers.*)

CHANDEL. Imagine—you haven't come to see me for months and months. I use your name for an alibi—and you barge into my home at the very moment you should have stayed away.

CASTILLO. How was I to know?

CHANDEL. What the devil! When a man hasn't seen a friend for a long time, the first question that should enter his mind is "am I being used as an albi?" Any fool should know that.

CASTILLO. What do you want of me? I'm not a fortune-teller.

CHANDEL. (*Standing, back to public, fastening trousers.*) No—you're no fortune-teller. There are some people who bring *mis*fortune with them, that's all. (*Folding the trousers he took off, puts them on piece* L. *of door.*) Well, what did you want to see me about?

CASTILLO. (*Sits* R. *of table.*) Perhaps you will find me a little indiscreet.

CHANDEL. (*Puts his coat on again, sits* L., *speaking between his teeth.*) I imagine so.

CASTILLO. I have made arrangements to meet the Police Inspector here.

CHANDEL. Here? In my home?

CASTILLO. You know I value your advice. But first, let me tell you good news. I caught my wife last night—in the act.

CHANDEL. But that means nothing unless you caught the lover.

CASTILLO. But we have the lover.

CHANDEL. Are you sure?

CASTILLO. Yes—it is a man named Roussel.

CHANDEL. Huh?

CASTILLO. He is a doctor.

CHANDEL. Did he admit it?

CASTILLO. Of course not—he denies it. But his pantalones— (*Pronounce: pahn-ta-lo-ness. Points to his own trousers.*) —his pantalones betray him. He left them when he ran away.

CHANDEL. (*With a look that speaks volumes.*) His trousers? No!

CASTILLO. Yes! Do you know this Roussel?

CHANDEL. (*Forcing a casual air.*) Me? Never met him. (BABETTE *enters.*)

BABETTE. Monsieur Roussel is here.

CHANDEL. (*Hand on forehead.*) I think I have a fever.

CASTILLO. Roussel?

CHANDEL. Huh? Yes.

CASTILLO. But why were you singing about not knowing him?

CHANDEL. (*With a disconcerting calm.*) Who said that?

CASTILLO. You—to me.

CHANDEL. I said that? Never!

CASTILLO. (*Rising.*) I asked you—do you know Roussel? You said, "No, I do not know Roussel."

CHANDEL. You said "Broussel"—not "Roussel."

CASTILLO. Did I say "Broussel?"

CHANDEL. That's what I thought you said—it amounts to the same thing.

CASTILLO. (*Raising his eyebrows.*) Then, this Roussel—?

CHANDEL. (*Quickly.*) No connection. This Roussel is my shirt-maker.

CASTILLO. Is he a good one?

CHANDEL. Excellent. (*He sees* ROUSSEL *enter, runs to him to ward off a faux-pas, comes down with him.*)

ROUSSEL. (*Oblivious of* CASTILLO.) You played me a pretty trick, didn't you?

CHANDEL. (*Low voice.*) Sh— Quiet! That's the husband.

ROUSSEL. (*Full voice.*) What? What did you say?

CHANDEL. (*Low.*) I said that's the husband. That's Castillo.

ROUSSEL. I'm very glad to know that's Castillo.

CHANDEL. (*Low.*) Not at all! Quiet! (*Aloud, laughing to cover up.*) How are things going?

ROUSSEL. You ought to know. I want you to tell me why you—

CHANDEL. (*Cutting him quickly, low.*) Later, later. I'll tell you.

CASTILLO. (*Drawing* CHANDEL *to him, low voice.*) You are very friendly with your chirtmaker.

CHANDEL. We went to school together. (*Full voice, and with a casual air.*) My dear Roussel, may I present Monsieur Castillo?

CASTILLO. A pleasure, Monsieur.

ROUSSEL. (*Distracted.*) You're too kind. (*To* CHANDEL.) Once more, I want to ask you why—

CHANDEL. (*Cutting him.*) I know you're in a hurry. I'll be with you in a moment. (*To* CASTILLO.) He's in a hurry. You don't mind, do you? Will you step in here, please. (*Tries to usher him into room,* L.)

CASTILLO. Wait just one moment, my friend.

CHANDEL. (*Not understanding his intention.*) What?

CASTILLO. I said to wait one moment. (*Passes in front of* CHANDEL *to go to* ROUSSEL.) Monsieur, I have something very important to say to you.

ROUSSEL. What is it?

CASTILLO. I have in mind to buy some chirts.

ROUSSEL. (*Not comprehending.*) Yes?

CASTILLO. Something in medium price, very conservative.

ROUSSEL. And what is that to me?

CASTILLO. How?

CHANDEL. (*Comes between them, pushing* CASTILLO *to* L.) Why does he care if you need shirts?

CASTILLO. He's a chirt-maker.

ROUSSEL. I'm not interested in shirts now—I'm interested in trousers—a pair that fit me exactly. (*To* CASTILLO.) But, Monsieur, I would like very much to have a little talk with you.

CASTILLO. Gladly.

CHANDEL. (*Struggling to keep them separated.*) No! No! (*Between them, pushes each away with his arms.*) We haven't time now!

ROUSSEL. (*Exasperated, goes to rear.*) Oh!

CASTILLO. (*Insistent.*) But Monsieur wishes to speak to me.

CHANDEL. (*Pushing him to the* L.) No—no—he'll talk for hours about shirts—it's an obsession. Some other time. Go in there!

CASTILLO. (*Over his shoulder.*) But why?

CHANDEL. (*Still pushing.*) Because he's going to take my measurements. (*Stops to give him the supreme argument.*) I'm going to be completely nude. Wait in there.

CASTILLO. (*Turning.*) But the inspector?

CHANDEL. (*Pivots him by shoulders.*) I'll call you when he comes. Go!

CASTILLO. Don't forget. (*He goes in door,* L.)

CHANDEL. (*Leans against door,* L.) What a day! (*Then, like a man ready for a new fight, speaks to* ROUSSEL *who has moved to extreme* R.) What did you want to tell me?

ROUSSEL. (*Moves towards him, step by step.*) You ask? I want my trousers. Where are my trousers?

CHANDEL. Is that all? Here they are. They're quite safe. (*Hands them to* ROUSSEL *who holds them to his breast like a newly found treasure, goes down* R. *of table.*)

ROUSSEL. Ah! And what about the objects in the pockets?

CHANDEL. (*Goes down* L. *of table.*) Do you think I'm a pickpocket?

ROUSSEL. Now—down to case history. (*Sarcastically.*) You conducted yourself very well last night.

CHANDEL. Me?

ROUSSEL. Do you know what your escapade caused?

CHANDEL. Yes—I was told. You were pinched in my place.

ROUSSEL. Yes—I was.

CHANDEL. What can I say, my friend? It's unfortunate, but it's better than if it had been me.

ROUSSEL. What's that? Better? Listen to me, my friend, I don't intend to pay for others' mistakes. You're going to get me out of this.

CHANDEL. Me? (*With a calm that brooks no reply.*) Not on your life!

ROUSSEL. Huh?

CHANDEL. Is it my fault you got pinched?

ROUSSEL. (*Not believing his ears.*) Oh!

CHANDEL. Listen to me: for the honor of a woman, I risked my neck—jumping through windows, and climbing on balconies. I saved the situation, and then you bungled everything by showing yourself in drawers to the police officers.

ROUSSEL. But you took my trousers!

CHANDEL. Why weren't you wearing them? This will teach you to run around in your underwear. What if the Medical Society hears about this?

ROUSSEL. Do you think that's the end of all this?

CHANDEL. I think nothing, my friend. I know only one thing: I was not caught. You were caught—so uncatch youself.

ROUSSEL. Well, of all the— (*He throws the trousers over one shoulder.*)

CHANDEL. Quiet—my wife! (YVONNE *has entered from* R., *carrying a magazine and papers. She goes toward desk, not bothering to notice anyone. She slams a magazine on the table in passing.*)

ROUSSEL. Bonjour, Madame.

YVONNE. Oh—it's you, Roussel? Bonjour. (*She sits at desk, puts away the other papers she brought.*)

CHANDEL. (*Like a little boy.*) Yvonne!

YVONNE. (*Over her shoulder, barking at him.*) What?

CHANDEL. Are you still angry with me?

YVONNE. (*Laughing.*) Me? I have other things on my mind. (*To* ROUSSEL.) Why do you have those trousers on your shoulder, Roussel? (CHANDEL *quivers.*)

ROUSSEL. These? Chandel just returned them to me.

YVONNE. (*To* CHANDEL, *rising.*) So you return Castillo's trousers to Roussel?

CHANDEL. No, no, no! I didn't return them to him. I just took them off and—well—not knowing where to put them, I threw them over his shoulder. But I'm going to take them back. (*He seizes the legs of the trousers which hang over* ROUSSEL'S *back.*)

ROUSSEL. No! No! (*He grabs the trousers by the other end.*)

CHANDEL. Give them to me!

ROUSSEL. I said "no"! (*They tug furiously at the trousers.*)

YVONNE. Let him have them, Roussel—since they belong to Castillo.

ROUSSEL. They belong to me. (*He tugs harder and at same time mouths the word "letter" to* YVONNE.)

CHANDEL. (*Low to* ROUSSEL.) Idiot!

ROUSSEL. There! (*With a violent tug, he pulls the trousers out of* CHANDEL'S *grasp. He rolls them and puts them on the fireplace.*)

CHANDEL. Yvonne—it's true—I can't lie. I'll tell you frankly—the trousers belong to Roussel.

Yvonne. At last! And the hunt? Admit that you lied about the hunt.

Chandel. I didn't go hunting with Castillo or anyone else.

Yvonne. Just as I thought. (Castillo *comes in from* L.)

Castillo. Did you forget me?

Chandel. No—but you can come in.

Castillo. Madame Chandel, I have been thinking of your question about the hunt. I will tell you the truce. Your husband and I have hunted many times together.

Chandel. Huh?

Yvonne. (*Laughing.*) Really?

Chandel. Shut up, Castillo! My wife knows very well that we have never hunted together—or alone. Why tell such lies?

Castillo. But, you—

Chandel. No! No! Go into the other room. (*Pushes him towards door.*)

Castillo. A man never knows on which foot to dance in this house.

Chandel. Then don't dance! Who asked you to dance?

Castillo. You will call me when the Inspector comes?

Chandel. Yes! Go inside!

Castillo. Tonto! Baboso! Cretino! (*He goes into door,* Chandel *turns to others.*)

Yvonne. Were those Spanish love words?

Chandel. I have never seen such a sun-stroke.

Yvonne. (*Leaning on table, trying to be unconcerned.*) Why does the Inspector want to see Castillo?

Chandel. (*Going to her.*) Nothing important. His wife was caught in the act.

Yvonne. With you?

Chandel. With me. (*Quickly catching himself.*) With me? What made you say that? Would the husband be here if it were I?

Yvonne. Then which mistress were you visiting last night?

CHANDEL. I was with no mistress.

YVONNE. Are you going to tell me more stories?

CHANDEL. I assure you, I have never had a mistress. Never! Isn't that right, Roussel?

ROUSSEL. (*Seated by fireplace, back almost to public.*) I don't know—I don't know.

CHANDEL. (*Between his teeth.*) Thanks.

YVONNE. Then why did you invent those hunting stories?

CHANDEL. Well—you see—I had a surprise for you.

YVONNE. What now?

CHANDEL. Word of honor! There was a little house on the seashore that I wanted to rent for you.

YVONNE. You wouldn't have been so crafty about a thing like that. There's a woman mixed up in those hunts —somewhere.

CHANDEL. No—a house, I tell you—a charming little house where we can go on weekends. No woman at all.

YVONNE. And all the time I was waiting—naive and confident. Because I'm an honest woman and a faithful wife. Isn't that true, Roussel?

ROUSSEL. Oh, yes, certainly.

CHANDEL. Me too! I'm a—I'm a— Right, Roussel?

ROUSSEL. Yes, yes, certainly.

YVONNE. I've never tried to cheat on my husband. Have I, Roussel?

ROUSSEL. Oh, no.

CHANDEL. And I've never dreamed of deceiving my wife. Have I, Roussel?

ROUSSEL. No—you're both models of fidelity.

BABETTE. (*Entering from rear.*) Monsieur Pierre is here.

ALL. Pierre! (*They freeze, looking alarmed.* BABETTE *lets* PIERRE *pass, then exits.*)

PIERRE. (*His arms crossed, and a mischievious look on his face.*) Tell me—what was going on at thirty-five Avenue Gambetta last night?

(YVONNE *and* ROUSSEL *cough loudly.* CHANDEL *leaps towards* PIERRE.)

CHANDEL. How are you, my nephew? (*He pulls him, as if to whisper to him, dragging him to* L. *of table, and below it.* YVONNE *and* ROUSSEL *try to grab* PIERRE *from other side, but they are too late. They go down* R. *of table and around it, to get to him.*)

YVONNE. Bonjour, Pierre! (*Grabs his hand and pulls him towards* R. CHANDEL *pulls on other arm. It is a tug of war.*) Stop pulling like that!

CHANDEL. But you're the one who is pulling.

YVONNE. Me?

CHANDEL. Yes—you. (*They continue to pull.* ROUSSEL *helps* YVONNE.)

YVONNE. Let go of him!

CHANDEL. Why don't you let go?

PIERRE. What's all this about? (CHANDEL *gives a jerk that makes* YVONNE *fall in a heap against* ROUSSEL. *He drags* PIERRE *down* L. *and whispers.*)

CHANDEL. Not a word about last night and I'll give you five hundred francs. (*He lets go of* PIERRE'S *arm, and* PIERRE, *who has been resisting, stumbles backwards.* YVONNE *grabs him, pulls him far* R. *and whispers.*)

YVONNE. Five hundred francs for your silence. (*She lets go of* PIERRE *and pushes him back towards* CHANDEL.)

PIERRE. (*Agreeably surprised.*) Well, well! Lucky Pierre! (*All four are now in a line facing front, not saying a word. Pierre can't figure things out.*)

CHANDEL. (*To* YVONNE.) You see—I let him go.

YVONNE. So did I.

CHANDEL. Oh, yes.

ROUSSEL. We let go when you did.

CHANDEL. Oh, yes. (*After a moment of silence, as if someone had spoken.*) What?

YVONNE. (*Surprised, she smiles.*) Nothing.

CHANDEL. Oh! I was thinking—

PIERRE. (*Looking at one and then the other.*) What's the matter with everyone?

CHANDEL. (*Taking a brash step to finish things.*) Well, Pierre, we've seen enough of you.

YVONNE and ROUSSEL. Yes, we've seen enough of you.

CHANDEL. Yes, we have to talk. Won't you come back later?

PIERRE. Glad to oblige. I'll go talk to Babette. See you later.

(PIERRE *leaves, rear. They are happy to be rid of him.* CHANDEL *is at* L. YVONNE *and* ROUSSEL *at* R. *They breathe easier, but a new crisis is written on their faces.* YVONNE *and* ROUSSEL *approach each other.* CHANDEL *puts his hand to his forehead. All this and what follows is played in place. Doorbell rings, and they all shudder.*)

CHANDEL. (*With a light air that fools no one.*) Some-one rang.

YVONNE. (*With little affirmative shakes of her head.*) Yes—someone rang.

ROUSSEL. (*Like a fifth wheel.*) Someone rang.

CHANDEL. (*After a pause.*) Who can it be?

YVONNE. (*With a gesture of hands meaning she doesn't know.*) Uh—uh—

ROUSSEL. I don't know.

BABETTE. (*Entering at rear.*) Inspector Duval is here.

CHANDEL. (*Without budging.*) It's Inspector Duval.

YVONNE. It's Inspector Duval.

ROUSSEL. It's Inspector Duval.

CHANDEL. (*To* YVONNE.) Do you know Inspector Duval?

YVONNE. No. Not at all. (*To* ROUSSEL.) Do you know Inspector Duval?

ROUSSEL. Never heard of him.

CHANDEL. I haven't either. (*To* BABETTE.) Show him in.

BABETTE. (*Opens door.*) Monsieur may come in now. (*She allows* DUVAL *to pass, and then exits.*)

DUVAL. (*He has a package under his arm.*) Messieurs! Madame!

CHANDEL, YVONNE, ROUSSEL. (*All turning together as* DUVAL *speaks.*) Inspector Duval!

DUVAL. (*Going to* CHANDEL.) Monsieur Chandel?

CHANDEL. Yes. I presume you're here about the Castillo affair. Monsieur Castillo is in the next room. I'll bring him in. Monsieur Roussel is already here. (*He goes towards door,* L.)

DUVAL. (*To* YVONNE.) And Madame Roussel, if I'm not mistaken? (CHANDEL *turns on hearing* DUVAL'S *words.*)

CHANDEL. Where is Madame Roussel? (*Sensing the situation.*) That's my wife—Madame Chandel.

DUVAL. She is?

YVONNE. Of course I am.

CHANDEL. Certainly. Monsieur Roussel has no wife.

DUVAL. Ah! (*He clears throat, throws back his head. He has caught on. Uttering a very sneaky laugh, he crosses down* R. *of table as* CHANDEL *goes out,* L.)

YVONNE. (*Crossing quickly to* DUVAL, *followed by* ROUSSEL.) Inspector, I'm going to explain.

ROUSSEL. It's very simple.

DUVAL. No need of that, Madame. As a magistrate, I am mute—and as a man of the world, I see nothing, hear nothing. (*He smiles, with a chivalrous gesture.*)

YVONNE. (*Relieved.*) Oh—you angel!

DUVAL. I'm professional, Madame—and I'm a Frenchman. (*He kisses her hand gallantly.* YVONNE *and* ROUSSEL *exchange a look of relief, as* DUVAL *goes to* R. *of table, puts his package on table, and* CHANDEL *enters from* L. *with* CASTILLO.)

CHANDEL. Here is Monsieur Castillo.

CASTILLO. Inspector, I asked you to come here because I wanted my good friend Chandel to learn the details of the affair.

CHANDEL. (*To* YVONNE.) You hear that?

DUVAL. And I wish to add that the accused in the case, who energetically denies his guilt, has assured me that the true culprit will be revealed here.

ROUSSEL. Perfectly said.

CASTILLO. What does this chirt-maker know about it?

CHANDEL. (*To* YVONNE.) My dear, this is a personal matter concerning Monsieur Castillo. If you care to leave—

CASTILLO. Not at all. Madame is not in the way. Please stay with us.

YVONNE. Thank you. I think I shall find it very interesting.

(CHANDEL *makes a grimace, sits in chair by desk.* YVONNE *is on chair near fireplace.* ROUSSEL, R. *of table.* CASTILLO *sits,* L. *of table.* DUVAL *is behind table.*)

DUVAL. Messieurs, I shall relate the facts. At the request of Monsieur Castillo, I surprised his wife last night in the act of adultery—flagrante delicto, as we say.

CASTILLO. Pardon me.

DUVAL. (*Annoyed.*) Monsieur?

CASTILLO. I compliment you. (*Seeing* DUVAL *look daggers at him.*) I'm the husband.

DUVAL. Monsieur Castillo, we know you're the husband. Please allow me to continue. The accomplice in this flagrant act had time to escape through the window—obviously in his under-garment—since we found his trousers in the room. I sent my men in pursuit. Five minutes later they returned with a man—without trousers—whom they found in an adjoining apartment. This man was Monsieur Roussel.

ROUSSEL. A mere coincidence. I'm the victim of a judicial error.

CASTILLO. (*Gives a cry of surprise.*) Ah! Then it *was* you.

ROUSSEL. Me? What?

CASTILLO. Never mind! (*Rises, goes to* CHANDEL.) You told me he made chirts.

CHANDEL. I didn't want to upset you at the time.

CASTILLO. He is no chirtmaker?

DUVAL. (*Thundering at* CASTILLO.) Monsieur Castillo!

CASTILLO. (*Cowering, sits again* L. *of table.*) He told me he made chirts.

DUVAL. As you see, Monsieur Roussel categorically denies the allegations formulated against him, and, in fact, I must say that certain circumstances seem to give credence to his denial. First of all, we had him try on the trousers which were found in the room. It is certain that these trousers were not made for him.

ROUSSEL. That's conclusive.

DUVAL. Moreover, we have here the supporting evidence. (*He takes the package from the table.*)

CHANDEL. (*Nervously, going to* DUVAL.) But that's useless. What will it serve? Why do you need to know the accomplice? You surprised Madame Castillo—you found the trousers with her—convincing proof that a man had been there. It seems to me that is sufficient.

CASTILLO. It's sufficient for me.

CHANDEL. And for me, too. (*Goes down near desk, sits.*)

DUVAL. Perhaps—perhaps. But not for the law! Finding a woman in a room, consorting with a pair of men's trousers, does not prove adultery. (*He unwraps package.*) We have here the article in question. (*They all rise, but do not move a step.*) All we need to do now is to find the owner of this garment. Any comment? (YVONNE *and* CHANDEL *exchange glances and mutter "no."*) The question is—how to find him?

CASTILLO. Ah, sí!

ROUSSEL. It's simple.

CHANDEL. But, Inspector Duval, how can you hope to find him? You can't stand in the street and try the garment on every man who passes. The case should be closed.

DUVAL. Monsieur Chandel, we do not close a case so easily. And I do not believe we shall have to look far for the man who owns these trousers. (*He goes around* R. *of table, faces* CHANDEL *who wipes his brow nervously.* ROUSSEL *grins at* YVONNE.) Monsieur Chandel— (*He approaches* CHANDEL, *holding up the trousers as if he wants him to try them on. At that moment,* PIERRE *interrupts with a breezy entrance, rear.*)

PIERRE. I'll bet you forgot all about me. (*Sees the trousers which* DUVAL *holds.*) Those belong to me. What are they doing here? (*There is a general murmur as* PIERRE *comes down* L. *of table towards* CHANDEL.)

CHANDEL. Did you hear? He said they belong to him.

PIERRE. Of course they do. (*Goes to* CHANDEL.) What's all this about?

CHANDEL. Nothing! Nothing! (*Whispering.*) Another five hundred if you don't change your story.

PIERRE. (*Turns towards* DUVAL.) My trousers! (*He crosses in front of table and takes the trousers from* DUVAL'S *hands.*)

DUVAL. Do you recognize those trousers as belonging to you?

PIERRE. More than ever!

DUVAL. You admit that you were at thirty-five Avenue Gambetta last night?

PIERRE. How did you know?

CHANDEL. He admits—did you hear?— He admits it.

PIERRE. Of course. Why not?

CHANDEL. There! It's settled.

DUVAL. What is your name, Monsieur?

PIERRE. Pierre Morillon. Why? (DUVAL *writes in his note-book.*)

DUVAL. May one ask why you were at thirty-five Avenue Gambetta last night?

PIERRE. Of course. I went to see my little woman.

YVONNE. (*Shocked.*) Oh! His little woman!

CASTILLO. Your little woman? You don't seem to suspect that she might also be mine.

PIERRE. Yours? (*Very surprised.*) Oh—it's the monkey!

ALL. The monkey?

PIERRE. The monkey that forced me to hide in the closet.

CASTILLO. (*Angry.*) I'll give you a monkey! (*Advances on* PIERRE *who hides behind* DUVAL.) Take note of that, Inspector.

PIERRE. Inspector?

CASTILLO. At least, now I can get my divorce.

PIERRE. Divorce? I thought you were just a friend.

CASTILLO. I am the husband, Monsieur!

PIERRE. But I didn't know she was married—believe me. I swear to you—she never told me she was married.

CASTILLO. That makes no difference. I know what I want to know and I can get my divorce. Thank you, Inspector. Thank you, Messieurs. Thank you, all. (*He goes out, rear.*)

PIERRE. (*Starting to follow.*) But, monsieur—

CHANDEL. Let him go!

PIERRE. But I want to explain— (*He runs out.*)

ROUSSEL. (*To* CHANDEL.) I don't understand this at all.

CHANDEL. Why try?

DUVAL. I see that my mission is accomplished. Monsieur Roussel, it remains for me to offer you my humble apology.

ROUSSEL. Not at all, Inspector, not at all.

DUVAL. Madame, I offer my respects. Monsieur Chandel—your humble servant.

CHANDEL. I'll see you to the door.

DUVAL. Please do. (*They go out together,* DUVAL *looking back and laughing knowingly.*)

ROUSSEL. Well—what do you think about that?

YVONNE. It doesn't change any of my ideas. He could

fool the Inspector, but not me. Meanwhile—while we're alone—give me my letter.

ROUSSEL. Oh, yes—my trousers. (*He goes to fireplace, takes the trousers and unrolls them on table. He declaims:*)
I found my trousers—a lucky chance;
Long live trousers and long live France!

YVONNE. Make poems later. My letter! (*They take the trousers by each side of waistband and both start rummaging the pockets.*) Remember? It was next to your heart.

ROUSSEL. (*Turning rear pocket inside-out.*) But it's not there now. Look in the other pockets. (*Each investigates a side pocket.*)

YVONNE. Handkerchief—that's all.

ROUSSEL. Wallet and coins—nothing more.

YVONNE. Look again. You must find my letter.

ROUSSEL. But there's no other place to look. (*Holds up one leg of trousers.*) You see—it's empty. (*Holds up the other leg.*) And this leg is empty. And all the pockets are inside-out.

YVONNE. It has to be there somewhere. (*They feverishly ransack again. Each puts an arm up one leg of the trousers.* CHANDEL *enters without their being aware. He comes between them, half hidden by the trousers.* YVONNE *and* ROUSSEL *look stupid.*)

CHANDEL. What is this—a game? Or, are you admiring the fabric? (YVONNE *and* ROUSSEL *slowly withdraw their arms from the trouser legs.*)

ROUSSEL. I was showing my trousers to your wife.

CHANDEL. That's interesting. I'm glad you're not in them. (*Changing tone.*) Well, my friends, you saw what happened. Our nephew Pierre is a wild one. Who would ever have suspected him? And with Madame Castillo!

YVONNE. (*Obviously not telling the truth.*) I wasn't surprised. Pierre confided in me some time ago about his relations with Madame Castillo.

CHANDEL. What?

YVONNE. Do you mean to say that you didn't know Pierre was in very deep with her?

CHANDEL. No!

YVONNE. The money he borrowed from *you* was spent on *her*.

CHANDEL. (*Suffocating, to audience.*) So! I was paying double.

YVONNE. But what really annoyed Pierre—the poor boy—was that there was also an *old man* involved with the woman.

CHANDEL. An old man? Who said that?

YVONNE. She did. To Pierre.

CHANDEL. An old man? It was just a manner of speaking. She couldn't possibly have said "an old man."

YVONNE. (*Sarcastic.*) Why are you so sure?

CHANDEL. Well—I mean—I mean— (*Angrily, he bursts out.*) I'm not an old man!

YVONNE. (*Hand on his shoulder.*) Ah! You?

CHANDEL. Huh? No—I mean to say—

ROUSSEL. (*Coming back from fireplace where he has put trousers.*) Careful, there—you're going to bury yourself.

CHANDEL. Go away—you annoy me.

YVONNE. I think you gave yourself away, my friend.

CHANDEL. No—no—I want to explain.

YVONNE. Why explain? You see I am very well informed. It was you who was with Madame Castillo last night. Why not admit it?

CHANDEL. (*At wits' end.*) Well—all right. I can see that my lies won't get me out of this. I prefer to face the truth. Yes, I was with Madame Castillo last night.

YVONNE. So—you've decided at last.

CHANDEL. You see—I just don't know how to lie.

YVONNE. (*Laughing, goes to* ROUSSEL, *pointing at* CHANDEL.) Did you hear that? He doesn't know how to lie. (*Back to* CHANDEL.) I think you wrote the text!

ROUSSEL. I believe my departure is indicated. (*Starts to go out.*)

YVONNE. No—no—you may stay. I want you to hear this. (*To* CHANDEL.) Everything is finished between us, Monsieur Chandel.

CHANDEL. (*Like a little boy.*) Oh, Yvonne—forgive me.

YVONNE. Never during this life.

CHANDEL. Now, see here! (*To* ROUSSEL.) Say something! Have you nothing to say about this?

ROUSSEL. Yes. (*To* YVONNE, *with profound indifference.*) Yvonne—let's look at it this way—

CHANDEL. You see! Listen to him! I swear that I will never see Madame Castillo again—never. Not her, nor any other woman.

YVONNE. That's easily said!

ROUSSEL. (*Mechanically, without realizing he is charging* CHANDEL.) Yes—that's easily said.

CHANDEL. Keep quiet—you—if that's all you can say. (*To* YVONNE.) I swear—no more infidelities—no more hares—no more rabbits—no more baskets. (*Suddenly, as if he has a great confession.*) Oh, yes—the baskets. I'm not forced to tell you this—but I will—the baskets came from the food shop. And to prove it, I'll show you the bill for the last one. (*He looks in several pockets and pulls out* YVONNE'S *letter on pink paper. Then a thought strikes him.*) Wait a minute! I remember now that I threw the bill in the fire so you wouldn't find it. What is this letter?

YVONNE. (*Shaken, leans to* ROUSSEL *and whispers.*) My letter!

ROUSSEL. Oh!

CHANDEL. (*Opens letter while* YVONNE *and* ROUSSEL *stand paralyzed.*) It's from you.

YVONNE. I know—I know. Give it to me. (*She tries to grab it but* CHANDEL *puts letter in other hand and pushes* YVONNE *away.*)

CHANDEL. Let me read it. (*Sits* R. *of table.*)

YVONNE. Why waste your time?

CHANDEL. But I want to read it. (*Reads aloud.*) "My friend—I have only one word to say: at this time there is no longer any obstacle between us." (*Looks up.*) "No obstacle between us." Why were you writing that to me?

YVONNE. (*Very embarrassed.*) Well—I don't know.

ROUSSEL. (*Intervening.*) Oh—it was one evening—

CHANDEL. What? Why are you mixing in? You couldn't possibly know about this. (*Starts reading again.*) "Free from myself, I engage myself to you." (*Crying out.*) Oh!

YVONNE and ROUSSEL. (*Trembling.*) What?

CHANDEL. (*Convincingly, rising as he speaks.*) I know!

YVONNE and ROUSSEL. (*Weakly.*) You know? (*They exchange glances.*)

CHANDEL. (*Very deliberately, like a man recalling a memory.*) Yes! It was one or two days before our engagement. (YVONNE *and* ROUSSEL *look at each other, confused as* CHANDEL *continues to read.*) "Understand that I act as I do because *he* wishes it." (*Looks up.*) Of course! "He"—that was your father!

ROUSSEL. (*With a sigh of relief.*) Really!

CHANDEL. (*With conviction.*) Yes! Yes indeed! (*With difficulty* YVONNE *and* ROUSSEL *restrain a laugh.*) You wouldn't believe it, but I didn't remember this letter at all.

YVONNE. (*With affected reproach.*) Oh! How can you say that?

CHANDEL. (*Quickly, as though he regrets his forgetfulness.*) Oh—but now I recall it very clearly. My dear, dear Yvonne—in memory of those wonderful days—in memory of the moment you wrote me this wonderful letter —please forgive me.

YVONNE. (*Looks him straight in the eye a moment.*) No! (*Crosses to* L., *near desk.*) I could never do that! No! No! Never! (PIERRE *enters from rear and comes down.*)

PIERRE. That man wouldn't listen to a word I said.

CHANDEL. Oh, Pierre—help me to soften your aunt's heart.

PIERRE. (*Not understanding.*) Me?

CHANDEL. Yvonne, I promise to be a model husband in the future.

ROUSSEL. (*Intervening.*) Forgive him, Yvonne.

CHANDEL. (*Gratefully, to* ROUSSEL.) Thank you, my friend.

ROUSSEL. He's guilty as the devil, but—

CHANDEL. Shut up!

YVONNE. No—I can never forgive you.

CHANDEL. (*Furious.*) Oh!

PIERRE. (*Low to* YVONNE *while* CHANDEL *argues with* ROUSSEL *at* R.) My dear aunt, permit me to insist.

YVONNE. It's useless.

PIERRE. (*Still lower voice.*) Forgive him—in the name of the woman who was at thirty-five Avenue Gambetta last night.

YVONNE. (*Confounded, she looks squarely at* PIERRE.) In the name of—? (*Decisively.*) So be it! (*Crosses to* CHANDEL.) I forgive you.

ROUSSEL and PIERRE. Ah!

YVONNE. But no hunting!

CHANDEL. (*Graciously, embracing* YVONNE.) If I hunt, it will only be for feathered or furred creatures.

ROUSSEL. Meanwhile, my dear friends—if you will kindly excuse me— (*Takes his trousers which are on fireplace.*) I shall take my drawers and go home. (*Picks up his hat, walks jauntily to door, then turns, grinning broadly.*) Au revoir! (*He goes out, humming "Under the Bridges of Paris."*) Poo-poo-poo-poo-poo—poo-poo-poo-poo-poo-poo.

CURTAIN

END OF PLAY

PROPERTY LIST

ACT ONE:
On table:
  seven empty cartridges
  bowl of shot
  bowl of powder with spoon
  bowl of wadding
  cartridge rammer
  crimper
  hammer
  cartridge pouch
embroidery basket on console up left
Roussel's cane and hat, up right, near door
On desk:
  pen and ink, writing paper, three books, some letters, blotters
under front leg of desk is a thin, red book of verse
shot gun (carried on by Chandel)
cleaning rag (carried on by Chandel)
wallet with ten 100-franc notes (carried on by Chandel)
telegram (carried on by Pierre)
note (carried on by Pierre)
old watch or travel clock (carried on by Pierre)
Break-away cane (carried on by Castillo)
Two-franc piece (carried on by Pierre)

ACT TWO:
On table:
  shrimp cocktails (can be fake)
  covered dishes
  bottle of Bordeaux wine
  butter in dish
  napkins
  tablecloth
  plates, glasses, silverware for two
  electric lamp
atomizer (carried on by Latour)
music on piano
cushions on sofa
blanket on bed

matches on fireplace, in container
key (carried on by Latour)
key (carried on by Roussel)
key (carried on by Pierre)
bottle of smelling salts (carried on by Chandel)
bottle of champagne (carried on by Roussel)
champagne cooler (carried on by Roussel)
Yvonne's letter (in Roussel's rear pants pocket)
note book and pencil (carried on by Duval)
gun case (brought in by Chandel)
5-franc coin (carried by Roussel)

ACT THREE:

basket (brought in by Chandel)
Bowls of pâté (in basket)
Chandel's trousers (brought in by Babette)
Yvonne's letter (in trousers which Chandel is first wearing)
Roussel's trousers (worn by Chandel at start of act)
Chandel's trousers (brought in by Duval, wrapped)
magazine (brought in by Yvonne)
handkerchief, wallet and coins (in pockets of trousers which
   Chandel takes off)
scissors (brought in by Yvonne)

Opening music for
THE HAPPY HUNTER
Words by Barnett Shaw
A.S.C.A.P.
Music based on an old tune
A HUNTING WE WILL GO !
Moderate March Tempo
(bugle or trumpet)
A hunt-ing we will go. I'm
off to catch a dear, a spec---ial kind of dear, the
dear---est lit--tle dear in all of gay Par---ee, oh,
she's the kind of dear I love to have quite near, the
on---ly kind of dear that has ap---peal for me. I find the
sport that a heal---thy man is need-ing,when I am lead-ing a hunt---er's
life, but in the name of the great out---doors I'm plead---ing: please
don't breathe a whis---per to my wife. I'm going to trap a fox, a
clev--er lit---tle fox, a ver---y craft-y fox that
lives in gay Par----ee, so let the fox be--ware, I'll
track her to her lair, and once we both are there, oh LA LA,youshould see
A hunt-ing we will go.

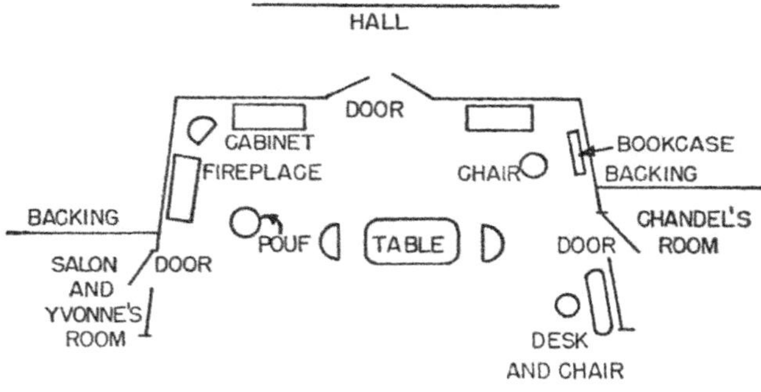

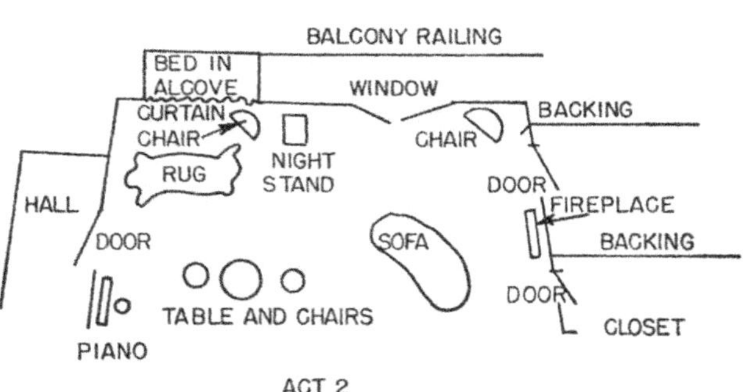

SCENE DESIGN
"THE HAPPY HUNTER"

www.ingramcontent.com/pod-product-compliance
Lightning Source LLC
Chambersburg PA
CBHW070344120726
47909CB00008B/2738